Laila Aurora Wright:

The L.A.W.

By

E.S. Bennett

Laila Aurora Wright:
The L.A.W.

FIRST EDITION MAY 2025

A MEGAVERSE CITY PUBLICATION

WWW.THEMEGAVERSECITY.COM

ISBN#979-8-218-99733-5

LIBRARY OF CONGRESS NUMBER

2025909153

COVER DESIGN BY E.S. BENNETT

COVER MODEL: *LORI A. WINDSOR*

Dedication;

This book is dedicated to the brave men and women of law enforcement and the military, those who serve and protect with unwavering courage and selflessness, often at great personal sacrifice. Their dedication to upholding justice, their commitment to safeguarding the innocent, and their resilience in the face of unimaginable challenges are a constant source of inspiration. Their stories, often untold, are the bedrock of this narrative, a testament to their strength, their unwavering resolve, and their profound impact on the world.

To the unsung heroes who risk their lives daily, who face danger head-on without hesitation, who make split-second decisions with profound consequences, this book is a humble tribute. Your sacrifices are not in vain; your dedication resonates deeply, shaping the fabric of our security and peace. This dedication is not only a gesture of gratitude but also a recognition of the extraordinary burdens you carry, the emotional tolls you endure, and the unwavering commitment you demonstrate every single day.

This book is also dedicated to those who have served alongside Laila, both real and imagined. The camaraderie, the shared experiences, the bonds forged in the crucible of adversity – these are the unseen threads that weave together the tapestry of courage and resilience. To the fallen comrades, their memories will forever burn brightly, a beacon of inspiration reminding us of the price of freedom and the importance of unwavering commitment. Their courage will always serve as a guiding light, reminding us of the strength within the human spirit and the power of selflessness. Furthermore, this dedication extends to the families and loved ones of those who serve. Their unwavering support, their steadfast faith, and their sacrifices are often unseen but undeniably crucial to the success and well-being of those in the line of fire. Their resilience and strength are testaments to the human spirit, supporting those who protect our communities and our nation. To the families who endure long periods of separation, uncertainty, and fear, this book is a small gesture of appreciation for your tireless support and unwavering dedication. Your sacrifices are as significant as those made by the men and women who wear the uniform or the badge. Your strength and steadfastness are what ultimately keeps hope burning in moments of adversity.

This book is dedicated to all of you – those who serve and those who support them – your courage, your resilience, and your unwavering dedication inspire us all.

Table of Contents

Laila's Return

The old farmhouse groaned under the weight of the Pennsylvania wind, a mournful sound that mirrored the ache in Laila's chest. Dust motes danced in the afternoon sunbeams slicing through the grimy windows, illuminating the quiet decay that had settled over the place since her father passed. Her mother moved out of the house after her father's funeral but now decided to return and asked if Laila would prepare the house for her mother and two brothers to return. The vacant farmhouse wasn't the comforting embrace she'd envisioned after the wreckage of her divorce from Frank. Instead, the familiar scent of woodsmoke and aging wood felt suffocating, a stark reminder of the life she'd left behind – a life of adrenaline-fueled missions, close calls, and the intoxicating camaraderie of the Forsvarets Special Kommando.

She ran a hand over the worn wooden table in the kitchen, the grain rough beneath her touch. Memories flickered – the biting cold of the Norwegian mountains, the sting of sweat and exertion during grueling training exercises, Frank's laughing face as he'd teased her about her competitive spirit. Now, those memories felt like phantom limbs, aching with absence. The laughter was a cruel echo in the oppressive silence of the farmhouse. The divorce had been brutal, a silent war fought with lawyers and accusations, leaving behind a trail of bitterness and unspoken resentments. The farm, meant to be a sanctuary, at this time felt more like a tomb.

The vast fields surrounding the house stretched out like a sea of green, rolling hills under the sky, the color of bruised plums. It was beautiful, undeniably so, but the beauty held no solace for her restless soul. The quiet was a constant pressure, a stark contrast to the cacophony of gunfire and screams she'd grown accustomed to. The solitude pressed in, a physical weight against her chest. She missed the comforting weight of her gear, the familiar feel of a weapon strapped to her thigh. The silence of the farm was deafening, the absence of purpose, agonizing.

She wondered what had possessed her mother to want to return here? Since her father's funeral, her mother seemed so lost, seemingly without purpose. Her father, Judge Henry Wright, was an honest man of strong character. He built this house as an oasis from the city, for the family and especially himself. Sitting on the State Supreme Court did take its toll on him. His sudden disbarment was equally stressful.

She moved through the house slowly, her steps echoing in the empty rooms. Dust lay thick on forgotten furniture, a layer of time settled over the neglected belongings. “Mom is going to be busy cleaning this place up”, she thought. Each object was a trigger, a portal to a past she couldn’t fully escape, even in this remote haven. A chipped porcelain doll, a reminder of her childhood innocence; a framed photograph of her ex-husband, Frank, capturing a fleeting moment of happiness that now felt like a lifetime ago. The memories were intrusive, relentless, clinging to her like the dust clinging to the old furniture.

The farmhouse held the ghosts of her younger family, but also the specters of her past missions. Images flashed: the faces of her fallen comrades, the terror in the eyes of the innocent caught in the crossfire, the cold precision with which she'd dispatched enemies. Even here, surrounded by the quiet of the countryside, the memories clung to her. The rural setting, so peaceful to others, underscored her internal conflict, creating a stark juxtaposition between her present reality and her past.

She found herself staring out the window, watching a lone hawk circle above the fields. Its flight was fluid, graceful, a stark contrast to the chaotic movements of her past life. She wondered if it too felt the weight of memories, the burden of experiences. It felt like a metaphor, the bird a symbol of freedom, something she had yet to regain. She was a creature of action, honed by years of rigorous training, molded by a life of calculated risk and intense focus. Now, the stillness and the quiet were a form of torture.

The weight of her past missions, both successful and those etched with loss, haunted her. The precision and calculated violence that had been essential to her work in Norway and beyond felt incongruous with the tranquility of the farm. The rhythmic ticking of the old grandfather clock in the hallway served as a constant, relentless reminder of the passage of time, each tick a hammer blow to her fractured sense of peace. It seemed to mock her attempts at finding solace.

She tried to find solace in familiar tasks, tending the neglected garden, cleaning the neglected rooms of the farmhouse, practicing yoga, but the chores provided little respite. The physical exertion, a routine she'd always relied on to ground her, offered only temporary relief. The effort only served to highlight her inner turmoil; the deep-seated feelings of loss, betrayal, and unfulfilled purpose festered beneath the surface. The rhythmic motions of weeding and cleaning served only to highlight her own emotional stagnation. She was a soldier, now a U.S. Marshal; she thrived in the midst of chaos, and this serene quiet was alien to her very being.

Later that evening, she received a call – an invitation to the funeral of a local police officer. It was an obligation, a small- town duty. She accepted, knowing that the quiet of the funeral would be an almost unbearable continuation of her personal quietude. But something in the way the Sheriff spoke, a subtle hesitation in his voice, pricked her attention. She had learned to sense subtleties, to read the unspoken language of tension, long ago in Norway, and even now, here on this quiet farm, those skills didn't sleep. The invitation, seemingly benign, felt charged, carrying the subtle weight of something hidden, a dangerous undercurrent beneath the surface.

Driving to the small town church, the contrast between the rolling hills and the neat, ordered rows of gravestones struck her. The stark order was a world away from the unpredictable chaos of her former life. The simple wooden crosses and neatly placed flowers were a symbol of a life lived, ended; a life that seemed so peaceful in contrast to her own inner turmoil. But as she arrived, and entered the church, the sense of quiet didn't feel peaceful; it felt stifling, heavy with the unspoken anxieties of the small town. The seemingly peaceful setting concealed something far more dangerous; and this awareness heightened her senses, preparing her for the confrontation to come. The subtle inconsistencies, the unspoken tension – these were the things she was trained to notice, the things that spoke volumes beyond the surface calm. And she noticed. The quiet of the Pennsylvania countryside was no match for her finely tuned senses. This was just the beginning. The homecoming had been anything but peaceful.

A Fallen Officer's Funeral

The scent of lilies and old wood hung heavy in the air, a cloying sweetness that did little to mask the underlying tension. Rows of somber faces, mostly familiar to Laila from the small-town gossip she'd overheard in the general store, filled the pews of the quaint church. Officer Miller, a man she'd seen occasionally patrolling the town square, lay in a polished mahogany coffin, his youthful face strangely serene despite the tragedy. The muted murmur of condolences filled the spaces between the hymns, a low hum that felt almost conspiratorial in its hushed intensity. But Laila, trained to read between the lines, heard more than quiet grief. She felt the undercurrent, a subtle tremor of unease that vibrated through the seemingly placid atmosphere.

It wasn't just the quiet; it was the *type* of quiet. The kind that clung to you like damp wool, a silence pregnant with unspoken words and half-hidden anxieties. The carefully controlled sorrow, the forced smiles exchanged between acquaintances – these were not the hallmarks of genuine grief in her experience. Years spent observing human behavior in high-stress situations had honed her perception to a razor's edge. She saw the subtle flinches, the averted gazes, the nervous readjustments of posture – all tiny signals that screamed of something concealed beneath the veneer of polite mourning.

Her gaze drifted to the honor guard, their faces stiff and unyielding, each movement precise and practiced. Yet, she detected a dissonance, a slight lag in synchronization between two of the officers, an almost imperceptible hesitation that spoke volumes. These were small things, easily overlooked, but to Laila, they were the telltale signs of a carefully constructed deception. The polished precision felt forced, almost theatrical, too perfect to be genuine. She'd seen enough staged events in her past to recognize the subtle tell-tales of fabrication. They were performing a role, not genuinely mourning their fallen comrade. And that, she knew instinctively, was wrong.

The Sheriff, a portly man with kind eyes that seemed to belie a hidden weariness, delivered the eulogy. His voice, though choked with emotion, lacked the raw agony she'd witnessed at other fallen officer funerals. It was a practiced performance, calculated and controlled. He spoke of Officer Miller's dedication, his bravery, his unwavering commitment to upholding the law. Beautiful words, eloquent and heartfelt, but Laila sensed a hollowness beneath the surface. It was as if he were reciting a script, not genuinely mourning his fallen friend.

During the recessional, as the mourners filed past the coffin to pay their final respects, Laila focused on the details. The floral arrangements, impeccably arranged, looked almost too pristine, too perfect. The way the light glinted off the brass nameplate on the coffin, the faint scent of something unfamiliar mixing with the lilies – it all felt off, deliberately staged to create a specific impression. This wasn't a natural outpouring of grief; this was a calculated display.

As she moved toward the open doors, allowing the crowd to precede her out into the bright Pennsylvania sunlight, her keen senses picked up on more inconsistencies. She noticed a slight tremor in the earth, a faint vibration that felt subtly wrong. The perfectly manicured lawn, usually an image of serenity, seemed to possess a subtle disharmony, a discord that subtly suggested underlying activity, a planned disruption of the otherwise serene scene. It was as if the very ground beneath her feet were humming with a hidden energy. She felt her instincts sharpen, her senses heightening, attuned to the nuances of the setting.

Stepping out of the church, the sharp contrast between the somber atmosphere within and the vibrant energy of the sunlight, striking. The sunny day felt incongruous with the shadow of death that hung over the town. The cheerful sounds of birdsong and the gentle breeze seemed mocking in their obliviousness to the underlying unease. But Laila felt the subtle unease, a tangible tension in the seemingly cheerful atmosphere.

The Sheriff approached her, his face creased with concern. “Tough day, Marshal,” he said, his voice low.

Laila nodded, her eyes scanning the crowd. "It is," she replied, her voice barely a whisper. She couldn't shake the feeling that something was amiss, a disquiet that resonated far deeper than simple grief.

The procession to the cemetery was a slow march, a somber parade of grief-stricken faces. But for Laila, the quiet procession was not a mournful tribute but a carefully orchestrated scene, a potential cover for something far more sinister. She noticed the subtle deviations from standard protocol, the unnaturally stiff posture of the pallbearers, the occasional furtive glances exchanged between some of the mourners. The details, minute and almost insignificant to the casual observer, painted a disturbing picture. She knew, with a certainty that chilled her to the bone, that something was not right. Something was deeply, dangerously wrong.

The cemetery was a landscape of ordered quiet, a stark contrast to the vibrant chaos she'd left behind in her previous life. The rows of gravestones, each one a testament to a life lived and concluded, seemed to represent the finality she was desperately trying to escape. The carefully placed flowers seemed almost too perfect, a manufactured display of grief, and this only heightened her suspicions. The pristine condition of the grounds, the precisely aligned markers – it all seemed too immaculate, almost contrived. Her gaze swept across the assembly, picking up on subtle inconsistencies, tiny discrepancies in posture and demeanor that wouldn't register with others, but were clear to her trained eyes.

As the coffin was lowered into the ground, a sudden gust of wind swept through the cemetery, rustling the leaves of the ancient oak trees that surrounded the burial site. The wind carried with it the faintest scent of gasoline. Laila's senses immediately focused on the subtle scent, her body reacting instinctively. The smell, barely perceptible to most, was clear to her, a potent indicator of something deeply disturbing. It was not the natural scent of a forest; it was the unmistakable odor of high-octane fuel, carefully placed to blend into the natural environment, masking its true purpose. And in that moment, she understood. The funeral wasn't just a funeral. It was a cover, a meticulously planned façade for something far more treacherous.

Her eyes scanned the faces of the mourners, each one now suspect in her eyes. She noted the subtle way one man, a tall figure with broad shoulders and a quiet intensity, kept glancing towards a nondescript van parked at the edge of the cemetery. The van was innocuous, blending into the background, seemingly unassuming, but Laila's senses had already identified it as the center of the unfolding drama. It was positioned strategically, partially obscured by the trees, its presence almost invisible, waiting patiently in the wings of a seemingly tragic occurrence. She sensed a cold, calculated precision that only a professional could execute so flawlessly.

The sheriff's words, the subtle inconsistencies in the mourners' behavior, the almost imperceptible tremors in the earth, the pristine condition of the cemetery, the carefully placed floral arrangements, the unnatural stillness of the wind before the sudden gust – all the pieces were falling into place. It was a puzzle box of deceit, and Laila, with her acute powers of observation and years of experience in deciphering hidden agendas, was beginning to unlock its secrets. This wasn't a simple mourning event; this was a meticulously planned operation, a stage set for an act of violence. The faint scent of gasoline was only the most obvious clue in this symphony of controlled chaos.

The Sheriff's carefully orchestrated eulogy, the unnatural stillness of the wind that preceded the brief gust carrying the scent of fuel – it was a cruel symphony of deception, a performance designed to cover the true nature of the event. Her instincts screamed at her, a cold, hard certainty that she wasn't attending a funeral, but witnessing the prelude to a much larger, far more sinister event. This wasn't just about the death of a police officer; it was about a calculated attack, a meticulously planned ambush. She was no longer just a former Ranger, a former Marshal; she was a woman who had seen too much, a woman who knew the difference between genuine grief and a perfectly orchestrated charade. And in this quiet, seemingly peaceful cemetery, she'd just witnessed the unveiling of a conspiracy that threatened the safety of many. The homecoming was far from over. It was just the beginning.

Unraveling the Conspiracy

The freshly turned earth still held the scent of gasoline, a phantom smell clinging to the damp soil. Laila, her gaze fixed on the nondescript van parked at the edge of the cemetery, felt a familiar surge of adrenaline. This wasn't just a gut feeling; it was the cold, hard certainty born from years of experience in high-stakes situations. The van, seemingly innocuous, was the key. Its strategic placement, the subtle way it blended into the landscape, spoke volumes. This wasn't a random act of violence; this was a meticulously planned operation.

She subtly withdrew from the immediate vicinity of the gravesite, her movements fluid and unnoticed. Years in the Army Rangers and as a U.S. Marshal had taught her the art of disappearing, of becoming a ghost in the crowd. She melted back into the throng of mourners, her eyes scanning for any further clues. The subdued chatter of the crowd was a constant background hum, but Laila's focus was laser-sharp, filtering out the noise and honing in on the relevant details. She watched as the Sheriff, his face etched with a carefully constructed sorrow, offered condolences to various individuals. His movements were rehearsed, his words carefully chosen. He was an actor on a stage, playing his part in this carefully orchestrated drama.

Her eyes fell on the tall man with broad shoulders she'd noticed earlier. He was talking to a woman with fiery red hair, their conversation hushed, their body language conspiratorial. Laila subtly adjusted her position, keeping them within her peripheral vision while appearing to observe the other mourners. She noted the way they kept glancing towards the van, their eyes darting quickly, as if checking to ensure it was still undetected. Their subtle nods and hand gestures confirmed her suspicion—they were communicating covertly, ensuring the plan was proceeding without a hitch. This wasn't simple grief; this was coordinated action.

Laila's mind raced, piecing together the fragments of information. The Sheriff's oddly controlled grief, the almost too-perfect floral arrangements, the tremor in the ground, the faint scent of gasoline, the unusual synchronization of the honor guard, the carefully placed van…it was all connected. It was a complex web of deceit, a sophisticated conspiracy woven with deadly precision. Her experience in Norway with Forsvarets Special Kommando, where she'd encountered similar tactics employed by extremist groups, flooded back. They operated with chilling efficiency, masking their true intentions with seemingly innocuous acts.

She needed more information. A quick check of her phone revealed no signal, a detail she immediately noted. The remote location of the cemetery, tucked away from the main town, explained it; they'd anticipated this. It was a strategic move to limit communication and disrupt any potential intervention. But Laila was prepared for this; she'd anticipated the lack of communication, and she was ready to operate independently.

She remembered the faint vibration she'd felt earlier. It wasn't a natural tremor; it was the subtle hum of a vehicle's engine, masked by the wind and the background noise. The van wasn't just parked; it was running, its engine idling patiently, ready for deployment. The carefully constructed scenario served as a perfect cover – an authentic-seeming funeral procession concealing a nefarious plot.

Her military training kicked in automatically. She assessed the terrain, calculating escape routes, identifying potential cover points, and mapping out tactical maneuvers. The cemetery, with its dense network of trees and uneven ground, offered ample opportunities for stealth and ambush. The neatly manicured lawns provided ample room for maneuverability. This wasn't just a simple investigation; it was a deadly game of cat and mouse, and Laila was determined to win.

Discreetly, she began to gather information. She approached the groundskeeper, a kindly old man who seemed oblivious to the true nature of the events unfolding around him.
Through carefully phrased questions, she learned about the van, confirming its presence wasn't usual for the cemetery. The groundskeeper only recalled seeing the van there a few times, always leaving quickly shortly after the cemetery was empty.

Next, she subtly questioned some of the mourners, using her charm and her trained ability to read body language to glean additional information. She discovered that the tall man with broad shoulders, a certain John Davies, according to the name tag on his suit jacket, was the owner of a local trucking company. That detail could be valuable. She also learned from a grieving widow, that the seemingly innocuous red- haired woman was John Davies' wife. Their seemingly happy marriage could potentially indicate shared complicity in this coordinated act of violence.

Laila's mind began to connect the dots. A trucking company…a van…a meticulously planned attack…it all pointed towards a coordinated effort involving transportation of weaponry and personnel. The domestic terrorist group was using the funeral as a decoy, a smoke screen for a larger operation. The targeted attack on law enforcement officers at

the funeral wasn't an end in itself; it was a diversion. There was something bigger at play, a far more sinister objective, hidden beneath the surface of mourning.

As the sun began to dip below the horizon, casting long shadows across the cemetery, Laila felt the weight of her responsibility. She was no longer just a bystander; she was the only one who could stop this. Her past experiences, her military training, and her sharp intuition were all converging towards a single point: a race against time to prevent a catastrophic act of terror. The seemingly peaceful homecoming was far from over. It was merely the prelude to a battle she was uniquely prepared to fight. The unraveling of the conspiracy had begun, and she wouldn't rest until the truth was revealed and justice served. The shadows were lengthening, but Laila Aurora Wright was ready to confront them.

The Fake Police Vehicle

The adrenaline, a familiar companion, pulsed in Laila's veins. The groundskeeper's words, casual yet revealing, echoed in her mind: "That van... it ain't usually around here. Seen it a couple times, always gone quick." Quick. The word hung in the air, a subtle clue to the urgency of the situation.
It wasn't just a van; it was a tool, a weapon carefully disguised as an ordinary vehicle.

Laila moved with the grace of a phantom, slipping away from the dwindling crowd of mourners. She circled back, keeping the van in her sights, her keen eyes meticulously scanning every detail. It was a nondescript white Ford Explorer, unremarkable at first glance. But Laila’s trained eye detected subtle anomalies. The paint job, while seemingly flawless, lacked the slight imperfections found on genuine police vehicles – the barely perceptible scratches, the faint discolorations from years of exposure to the elements. This was too perfect, too pristine. It screamed fabrication.

She moved closer, her heart pounding a steady rhythm against her ribs. The scent of gasoline was stronger here, mingling with the damp earth and the lingering smell of freshly cut flowers. She crouched low, her hand instinctively reaching for the Glock 17 holstered at her hip. Her fingers traced the cool metal, a comforting weight in her palm. Security, even in a seemingly safe environment, was never guaranteed.

A closer inspection revealed more discrepancies. The lettering on the side, identifying it as a police vehicle, was slightly off-center, the font a shade too bold, the spacing uneven. The emergency lights, while present, seemed strangely dull, lacking the vibrant intensity of authentic police equipment. The tires were new, almost aggressively new, with no sign of wear or tear, suggesting the vehicle hadn't seen much road time. These were not the subtle marks of age and service; these were deliberate omissions, calculated imperfections crafted to create an illusion of authenticity.

Laila's mind worked with the methodical precision of a finely tuned machine. She noticed the license plate, a seemingly official number from a neighboring state, meticulously forged but still carrying a faint trace of imperfection in the paint. A quick mental cross-reference with her memory banks – an extensive database of vehicle identification numbers and police equipment specifications from her time with the Marshals Service – confirmed her suspicions: this was no genuine police vehicle. This was a meticulously crafted deception, a wolf in sheep's clothing.

She examined the vehicle's undercarriage. There were no visible modifications, no obvious weaponry or explosives. But Laila knew the terrorists were too sophisticated to leave such obvious markers. Their expertise went far beyond simple vehicle fabrication; their actions demonstrated a level of planning and execution that bordered on artistry. They'd carefully selected a vehicle that wouldn't raise suspicions, one that seamlessly blended into the backdrop of the event.
The Ford Explorer was a common sight; its presence wouldn't be unusual in a rural setting, or even among law enforcement officers at a funeral.

Then, Laila noticed a barely perceptible weld near the rear bumper, a seam too perfect to be factory-made. She ran her fingers along it, her touch sensitive and sure. It was a hidden compartment, cleverly concealed. This was where the weapons, explosives, or whatever other deadly devices were likely hidden. A chilling realization gripped her: the terrorists were planning to use the fake police vehicle to gain the trust of attending law enforcement, ensuring close proximity for maximum impact. A seemingly innocuous police vehicle was, in actuality, a mobile killing machine.

She took out her small, high-powered tactical flashlight and shined it into the compartment, revealing a slight gap. With a small, almost silent pry tool from her kit, she carefully pried the compartment open. Inside, she found what she'd feared: a small arsenal of weapons and explosives meticulously wrapped in industrial plastic to avoid detection. A variety of assault rifles, several handguns with silencers attached and plastic explosives strategically placed within the space, made it clear what the terrorists intended. The sophistication of their setup spoke volumes about their level of planning and commitment to the mission. This wasn't an amateur operation; these were seasoned professionals. The level of precision in the construction of the fake police vehicle mirrored the meticulous planning of the entire operation.

The explosives were surprisingly sophisticated, not the crude homemade bombs she'd encountered in previous cases.

These were professional-grade explosives, carefully constructed to maximize damage and minimize risk of detection. She recognized the markings on the explosives: they matched a particular type known for its high potency and ease of detonation, used by several foreign terrorist organizations, but never before seen in a domestic operation. It was evident this terrorist group had access to advanced weaponry and expertise beyond the resources of typical domestic groups, which suggested either outside funding or training. This meant this operation was bigger and more complex than she initially thought.

The sheer audacity of it staggered her. They were using a funeral, a symbol of mourning and respect, as a cover for a planned massacre. The fact that they were not only willing to exploit the occasion but to deceive the law enforcement officers who were supposed to be protecting the public was a new low, even for her hardened standards. The methodical precision of their plan, their ability to manipulate the event with such chilling calculation, underscored the lethality of the situation. The terrorists were counting on the police's inherent trust in one another, that they would not scrutinize a seemingly fellow officer in mourning.

Laila carefully documented everything, taking detailed photographs with her high-resolution camera phone, which had just picked up enough signal to activate. She knew this evidence would be crucial in apprehending the terrorists and preventing the planned attack. The images would provide irrefutable proof, showing the intricate details of the fake police vehicle, the sophisticated explosives and weaponry hidden within, and the meticulous planning that went into the operation. This was not just a matter of stopping a group of terrorists; it was about exposing a deeply insidious plot with connections that went far beyond the confines of the small Pennsylvania town. The evidence was clear: this wasn't just a local threat; it reached far beyond her hometown. The scope of the conspiracy reached far beyond what she could have imagined, making the situation even more critical.

Her mind raced, trying to anticipate their next move, their ultimate objective. The funeral was a diversion; what was the real target? Was this a larger-scale attack planned for the near future? This meticulously planned assault on law enforcement at the funeral was a critical component of a much larger operation, a distraction to shield the terrorists' true actions. The implications were staggering: the nation's security and its citizens lives were in immediate jeopardy. The discovery of the fake police vehicle was just the tip of the iceberg. The plot was far deeper, more dangerous than she'd initially assessed. The shadows were closing in, but Laila was more determined than ever to expose the truth and stop these terrorists before they could strike again. The homecoming, far from being peaceful, had just become a deadly game of cat and mouse. And Laila, as always, was ready to play.

Preparing for Confrontation

The cold steel of her Glock 17 felt reassuring against her hip, a familiar weight in the growing darkness. The adrenaline, no longer a pulsing thrum, had settled into a steady, focused hum. Laila wasn't just reacting; she was calculating, planning, anticipating. Her mind, a battle-hardened strategist's tool, was already several steps ahead, mapping out potential scenarios, analyzing variables, assessing risks. The discovery of the bomb-laden fake police vehicle was just the beginning; the real confrontation was yet to come.

Her first priority was securing the evidence. The photographs she'd taken were crucial, but she needed more. She meticulously documented the vehicle's location using GPS coordinates, noting the surrounding landmarks and potential escape routes. Her training kicked in, instinctively analyzing the terrain – the cover, the concealment, the lines of sight. She identified potential ambush points and escape routes, both for herself and, more importantly, for the terrorists. Understanding their likely escape routes was paramount to intercepting them.

She knew the terrorists wouldn't stay. They wouldn't leave this evidence behind. They were professionals, not amateurs; their response would be swift and calculated, their escape route pre-planned. Laila needed to be faster, smarter. She had to anticipate their actions, anticipate their reactions to her discovery. This wasn't about a simple arrest; this was a high-stakes game of chess, where one wrong move could mean the difference between life and death, not just for her, but for countless others. The stakes were too high for a single miscalculation.

Her next move was to discreetly alert her superiors. She couldn't risk a direct call; it would be too risky, too easily traceable. Instead, she used a heavily encrypted messaging app, a secure communication channel reserved for sensitive operations, to send a concise, coded message to her former Marshal's Service contact, a trusted colleague she still maintained a clandestine connection with. The message contained only essential information: location, vehicle description, and the nature of the explosives. She avoided unnecessary details, minimizing the risk of interception. The coded message, a carefully crafted sequence of seemingly random words and numbers, would only make sense to someone with the right decryption key. She meticulously removed all metadata from the message to ensure it could not be traced back to her.

While waiting for a response, she focused on formulating a plan of action. She mentally reviewed several scenarios, playing them out in her mind like a seasoned chess master. Each move was calculated, each counter-move considered. She visualized the terrain, imagining the terrorists' movements, anticipating their reactions to her potential actions. This wasn't simply about apprehending them; it was about doing so safely, minimizing risk to civilian lives. She knew she couldn't afford a direct confrontation; their firepower exceeded hers significantly, even with her Glock.

She needed backup, but she couldn't rely on conventional methods. The local police force was still unaware of the situation, and contacting them directly would risk alerting the terrorists, giving them a chance to escape, or even to trigger the explosives. She had to find a way to secure the perimeter, contain the threat, and apprehend the terrorists without causing any unnecessary bloodshed or panic. That meant using stealth, intelligence, and her superior tactical knowledge to her advantage.

Laila's time in the Army Rangers, followed by her years as a
U.S. Marshal, had honed her skills to a razor's edge. She wasn't just physically fit; she was mentally sharp, her mind a well-oiled machine, capable of processing information, analyzing situations, and making split-second decisions under extreme pressure. Her experience in covert operations allowed her to recognize the intricate planning behind the terrorists' actions. This was not some hastily assembled operation; it was meticulously planned, calculated, and carried out by individuals who understood the importance of precision.

She used her tactical knowledge to find several vantage points around the van, positions that provided her with excellent visibility and concealment. She scanned the area for any signs of surveillance, looking for anything that would indicate the terrorists were monitoring her activities. She knew they'd be watching, waiting for her next move.
She needed to stay ahead of the game, anticipate their actions and counter them. This was about anticipating their next move and countering them effectively. She was preparing for an unconventional conflict that required a similar approach.

Her training was paying off, as she

systematically reviewed the area. Her past experiences flooded her memories, showing her how to anticipate the enemy's movements, as well as prepare her escape routes. Her calm demeanor masked the adrenaline pumping through her veins, allowing her to focus on the task at hand.

The silence of the night was broken only by the occasional chirping of crickets, a stark contrast to the adrenaline coursing through her veins. The weight of the situation bore down on her, the realization of the potential loss of life if she failed to stop these terrorists. Yet, fear was a luxury she couldn't afford. It was a time for action, for precision, for calculated risk. The coming confrontation wasn't just a fight; it was a test of her skills, her courage, her unwavering commitment to justice.

The encrypted message sent, Laila waited, her senses heightened, her awareness expanded to encompass every sound, every shadow, every subtle shift in the night's stillness. She had laid the groundwork, setting the stage for a confrontation that would demand everything she had – her skills, her experience, her resolve. The homecoming had turned into a battle, and Laila Aurora Wright was ready to fight. She was not simply a former soldier and marshal; she was a warrior, prepared to face any challenge. The next phase would determine the fate of many, and Laila was ready to accept the challenge. The weight of the situation did not diminish her resolve; instead, it fueled her determination.

She started mentally preparing for several scenarios, picturing how she would react in each situation. Her plan would depend on several factors, such as the number of terrorists and the equipment they had. She would need to analyze their reaction to her discovery, the possibility of reinforcements, and their escape plan. She had to be prepared to adapt to any situation.

The arrival of backup wasn't a guaranteed solution, as it could also alert the terrorists. She envisioned several ways of securing the perimeter, focusing on methods that would minimize the risk of detection. She could use her military knowledge to create a hidden perimeter, using the shadows and terrain to her advantage. The rural setting provided her with an advantage, as it allowed her to blend in with her surroundings and approach the situation from an unexpected angle.

Laila had identified several escape routes that the terrorists might use, and she mentally mapped out ways to intercept them or anticipate their escape. This involved utilizing the local geography and knowledge of potential hiding spots. Her familiarity with rural terrains would allow her to use the natural obstacles to her advantage in anticipation of a potential confrontation.

Her keen eyes scanned the area, constantly searching for any signs of movement or disturbances. She noticed several details that she had missed earlier: small tracks in the mud, footprints near the bushes, subtle vibrations in the ground that could be an indication of presence. Her past experiences came into play, as she was able to use her observation skills to recognize small details that would help her in anticipation of the enemy's arrival.

Her mind raced, formulating multiple strategies depending on the arrival of reinforcements and the terrorists' reactions. Each scenario she envisioned included methods of neutralization, escape routes, and backup plans, anticipating their countermeasures. Laila's mental agility allowed her to think ahead of the terrorists, anticipating their possible moves and adjusting her strategy accordingly. Her mind raced, preparing for the coming confrontation. This wasn't just a tactical operation; it was a battle of wits, a dance of shadows, where one false step could mean the end. And Laila was ready to lead.

Gathering Intelligence

The coded message sent, a weight lifted slightly from her shoulders, yet the pressure remained immense. Laila knew she couldn't rely solely on her former colleagues; she needed more information, more context. This wasn't just about stopping a bomb; it was about dismantling an entire operation, understanding its roots, its players, its ultimate goal. Her years as a Marshal had taught her the importance of meticulous intelligence gathering. She needed to know who she was facing, what their capabilities were, and what their next move would be.

Her phone, a seemingly innocuous device, was in reality a gateway to a clandestine network of contacts – former colleagues, informants, even a few individuals who operated in the grey areas between law enforcement and the shadowy world of intelligence. She carefully selected her contacts, each one chosen for their specific area of expertise, their access to information, and their trustworthiness. She couldn't afford leaks, couldn't afford betrayals. The stakes were too high.

First, she reached out to Marcus, a former

colleague from her time in the Marshal's Service. Marcus specialized in cyber intelligence, his expertise in tracking online activity and digital footprints invaluable in identifying potential terrorist networks. Their communication was encrypted, of course, a series of carefully worded messages that only they could understand. She provided him with the limited information she had – the vehicle description, the location, the type of explosives – and requested any information he could gather on similar incidents, any potential links to

known terrorist groups, or any digital breadcrumbs that might lead to the perpetrators.

Marcus's response was swift and efficient, a stream of data flowing through the encrypted channel. He had already identified several potential suspects, individuals with known extremist affiliations and a history of involvement in similar incidents. He provided links to their online activities, their social media profiles, their communication patterns, a digital tapestry woven from seemingly innocuous data points. Each link, each piece of information, served as a piece of the puzzle, slowly bringing the picture into sharper focus. Laila carefully analyzed the data, piecing together the fragmented information, forming a clearer picture of the individuals she was hunting.

Next, she contacted Isabella, an old friend from her time in Norway with the Forsvarets Specialkommando. Isabella had connections in various intelligence agencies across Europe, access to information that wouldn't be available through official channels. She provided Isabella with the same basic information, adding a request for any links to international terrorist organizations, any known connections to foreign funding, or any patterns in their operational methods.

Isabella's response was less immediate, the information she possessed more sensitive, requiring a higher level of discretion. She relayed information about a shadowy organization known only as "The Serpent's Fang," a group with suspected ties to various extremist factions across the globe. The details were scarce, shrouded in secrecy, but the links to the suspects Marcus had identified were undeniable. Isabella warned her that The Serpent's Fang was incredibly well-organized, exceptionally well-funded, and highly skilled in deception and counter-intelligence. This wasn't just a domestic threat; it was part of a much larger, more sinister operation.

With information from both Marcus and Isabella, Laila started to piece together a more comprehensive picture of the terrorist group. They weren't a ragtag bunch of amateurs; they were highly organized, well-funded, and expertly trained. Their operational methods were sophisticated, their communication encrypted, and their escape routes meticulously planned. She realized she was dealing with a network, not just a small cell of operatives.

The weight of the responsibility settled upon her, the enormity of the task ahead. This wasn't just about stopping a bomb; it was about dismantling a network, preventing a potential catastrophic event. She had to be meticulous, careful, precise. One wrong move, one misplaced step, and the entire operation could be compromised.

Using the information gathered, Laila started building a detailed profile of each suspect, outlining their strengths, weaknesses, and potential motivations. She studied their movements, their online activity, their connections, piecing together a tapestry of their lives, their routines, their habits. The more she knew about them, the better prepared she would be to anticipate their actions and counter their moves. She reviewed their known associates, looking for any potential weaknesses or vulnerabilities that could be exploited.

Her analysis revealed a pattern: the suspects all had military experience, many serving in special forces units. They were highly disciplined, highly skilled, and extremely dangerous. Their operational methods indicated a level of expertise rarely seen in domestic terrorist groups. This wasn't the work of amateurs; this was the work of professionals, individuals who understood tactics, strategy, and the importance of precision. This was a coordinated attack, a carefully planned operation, designed to inflict maximum damage.

Laila knew she couldn't tackle this alone. The sheer scale of the operation required a coordinated effort, a collaboration between law enforcement, intelligence agencies, and potentially even international partners. She had to find a way to pass on the information she had gathered, to alert the appropriate authorities, without compromising her sources or jeopardizing her own safety. She knew the risks were significant, but the potential rewards – preventing a massive terrorist attack – were even greater.

Her next move was carefully planned. She contacted her old contact within the FBI, a man named Robert Miller, a seasoned counter-terrorism agent who had a reputation for discretion and efficiency. She used a secure communication channel, a heavily encrypted line dedicated to sensitive operations, to relay the information she had gathered. She carefully crafted her message, selecting only the essential details, avoiding anything that could compromise her sources or expose her methods.

Miller's response was immediate. He confirmed the validity of her information, acknowledging the seriousness of the threat. He promised a swift and decisive response, a coordinated operation involving multiple agencies. It wouldn't be easy, he warned. The Serpent's Fang was a formidable enemy, but they had the resources, the expertise, and the determination to stop them.

With the information relayed, Laila continued her own investigation, keeping a watchful eye on the suspects' movements, anticipating their next move. She knew this was far from over; this was merely the beginning of a long, dangerous game. The ticking clock was still counting down, and the fight for justice was far from won. But Laila Aurora Wright was ready. She had faced down enemies before, and she would face them again. The weight of responsibility, the pressure of the situation, fueled her resolve, sharpening her focus, enhancing her determination. This was a battle she was prepared to fight, and she would win. The hunt was on, and the hunt was personal.

Profiling the Enemy

The intelligence from Marcus and Isabella painted a disturbing picture. These weren't disgruntled loners lashing out; this was a coordinated, highly skilled operation. The Serpent's Fang, as Isabella had called them, wasn't a new player on the scene. Their history, pieced together from fragmented intelligence reports, suggested a long, shadowy history of meticulously planned attacks, each one devastating in its own right. They were experts at blending in, at disappearing without a trace, leaving behind only devastation and a trail of unanswered questions.

Laila's years in the military, coupled with her time as a U.S. Marshal, gave her a unique perspective. She understood the meticulous planning that went into such operations. Every detail, every seemingly insignificant choice, had a purpose, a strategic reason. She had seen firsthand the chilling efficiency of well-trained operatives, their ability to anticipate and neutralize threats before they even materialized. This wasn't a game of chance; it was a game of chess played on a global scale, with the lives of countless innocents as the stakes.

Her small farmhouse, once a refuge from the chaos of her life, now became her operational base. Surrounded by the familiar scent of earth and the quiet hum of rural life, she delved into the mountain of data she had gathered. Spread across her kitchen table, maps, photographs, intelligence reports, and printouts of social media activity formed a chaotic yet organized battlefield. She worked tirelessly, fueled by black coffee and an unwavering resolve. Sleep became a luxury she couldn't afford, her mind relentlessly piecing together the puzzle, creating profiles of each suspect, connecting the dots, and anticipating their next move.

The first profile was of a man named Anton Volkov. His military record showed service with the Russian Spetsnaz, a unit known for its ruthless efficiency and its expertise in unconventional warfare. He was a master of disguise, skilled in close-quarters combat, and a master strategist. His online activity suggested a deep-seated hatred of law enforcement, fueled by a personal vendetta against a perceived injustice in his past. Laila suspected this fueled his involvement in The Serpent's Fang. His social media footprint was meticulously scrubbed, a ghost in the digital world, but she found a single, fleeting comment on a far-right extremist website, a subtle hint at his involvement.

The next profile was of a woman named Anya Petrova, a former member of the Israeli Defence Forces' elite Duvdevan unit. Her skills were legendary; her ability to adapt and overcome challenges was unmatched. Unlike Volkov, Petrova operated more in the shadows, a logistical mastermind, handling the group's finances and communication networks. She was a master of deception, capable of manipulating individuals and systems to achieve her goals. Her online presence was almost non-existent, making her even more dangerous. But Laila noticed an anomaly in her financial transactions, a small, almost insignificant deposit from an offshore account, a possible connection to foreign funding.

Then there was Dmitri Sokolov, a former operative with the GRU, Russia's military intelligence agency. He was the group's technical expert, a genius-level hacker with a knack for exploiting vulnerabilities in security systems. He was skilled in creating and deploying explosives, his online activity showcasing an unsettling fascination with advanced weaponry and unconventional tactics. Laila found evidence of his involvement in developing and deploying sophisticated surveillance systems used by the group. His seemingly innocuous blog posts on technological advancements masked a far more sinister purpose.

Laila carefully constructed profiles for each individual, outlining their skills, weaknesses, motivations, and potential targets. She considered their operational style, their communication patterns, their potential escape routes. She sought any vulnerabilities, any cracks in their armor, any personal weaknesses that could be exploited. She wasn't just building profiles; she was crafting a strategy, developing a plan to dismantle the entire operation.

Her analysis revealed a disturbing pattern. Each member possessed highly specialized skills, complementing each other perfectly. They were not just a group; they were a finely tuned machine, designed for maximum impact. Their meticulous planning, their expertise in surveillance and counter-surveillance, and their seemingly flawless execution pointed to years of experience and a frightening level of coordination.

Laila knew she couldn't go after them directly.

She needed a coordinated effort, a strategic approach involving multiple agencies. The FBI was already mobilized, thanks to her contact, Robert Miller. But she needed to provide them with more than just names; she needed to give them a roadmap, a detailed strategy to neutralize the threat without alerting the suspects. She needed to anticipate their every move, to stay one step ahead.

She began to focus on the overarching strategy of The Serpent's Fang. Her analysis showed their operations weren't random; they targeted symbols of power, places where maximum chaos could be inflicted. They didn't just want to kill; they wanted to create widespread panic, to sow discord, and destabilize society.

This realization sharpened her focus. She had to identify their next target. She analyzed the timing of their previous attacks, looking for patterns, for clues, for hints of their future plans. She cross-referenced the suspects' movements with potential targets, looking for connections, overlaps, and correlations.

The weight of responsibility pressed down on her, a crushing burden. The ticking clock was relentless, each second bringing the threat closer. But Laila wasn't one to back down. She had faced down death before, faced overwhelming odds, and emerged victorious. Her years in the military had forged her into an instrument of precision, a force of nature capable of facing unimaginable challenges.

With a renewed sense of purpose, Laila continued to refine her profiles, adding new details, and expanding her strategy. She was a lone wolf, but she was a wolf with a plan, a meticulous strategy, and an unwavering determination. The fight for justice was far from over, but Laila Aurora Wright was ready. The hunt was personal, and she would not rest until every member of The Serpent's Fang was brought to justice. The ticking clock was her only enemy, and she would outmaneuver it. She would win.

The Target Identified

The relentless ticking of the clock was a constant companion, a physical manifestation of the dwindling time Laila had to stop the impending catastrophe. Her analysis of The Serpent's Fang's past operations, their meticulous planning, and their chilling efficiency, had led her to a terrifying conclusion: their targets weren't random. They weren't simply choosing locations for maximum casualties; they were targeting symbols of American power, places that would trigger widespread panic and sow discord. This wasn't just terrorism; it was a carefully orchestrated campaign of destabilization.

Days bled into nights as Laila poured over intelligence reports, satellite imagery, and social media feeds, searching for a pattern, a clue, a hint that would reveal their next target. She meticulously cross-referenced Anton Volkov's movements with potential high-profile events, noting his proximity to Washington D.C. during the previous week. Anya Petrova's financial transactions revealed a sudden surge in activity originating from an account linked to a high-ranking official within the Department of Homeland Security, though the

connection was tenuous at best.
Meanwhile, Dmitri Sokolov's hacking activity seemed to center on securing access to the secure network of a major government building.

The pieces of the puzzle were slowly coming together, but the picture was still frustratingly incomplete. Laila knew she needed a breakthrough, a decisive piece of intelligence that would unveil the Serpent's Fang's intended target. The weight of responsibility pressed heavily upon her shoulders. She was a lone wolf, operating outside the conventional channels of law enforcement, but the lives of countless innocents hung in the balance, depending on her ability to decipher their plan before it was too late.

Frustration gnawed at her. The hours were ticking away. She needed a fresh perspective, a new approach. She grabbed a fresh cup of coffee, the bitter brew a stark reminder of the grim reality she faced. Her gaze fell upon a map of the United States pinned to her kitchen wall. She'd been focusing too much on the individual members of the cell and their digital footprints, neglecting the bigger picture. She needed to look at their potential targets through a broader lens, considering their capabilities and likely motivations.

Laila retraced the history of The Serpent's Fang, examining the geographical location and the symbolic significance of their previous attacks. Each location, initially seemingly random, now revealed a chilling pattern: high-profile events, symbols of American power and unity, meticulously chosen to maximize the impact of their attacks and the resulting chaos. They weren't just interested in killing; they wanted to cause widespread societal disruption, and they seemed to thrive on the ensuing chaos.

The realization struck her like a lightning bolt: the upcoming National Remembrance Day ceremony in Washington, D.C. The event, held annually to honor fallen law enforcement officers, was the perfect target. It was a symbolic representation of everything The Serpent's Fang despised – law and order, unity, and the very fabric of society. The sheer number of law enforcement officials attending would guarantee a significant death toll, and the symbolic nature of the event would make the attack all the more impactful.

The thought sent a chill down Laila's spine. The sheer scale of the potential catastrophe solidified her resolve. This wasn't just a terrorist attack; it was an act of war against the very foundation of American democracy. It was a carefully orchestrated attempt to instill fear and undermine public trust. And Laila was the only one who could stop it.

She immediately alerted Robert Miller at the FBI, relaying her findings. Her voice was calm, precise, devoid of emotion, a testament to her years of training. She laid out her evidence: the pattern of attacks, the symbolism of the National Remembrance Day ceremony, and the potential motivations of The Serpent's Fang. Miller listened intently, his usually jovial demeanor replaced with a grave seriousness. He confirmed that the FBI had been monitoring the group but lacked concrete evidence to justify a full-scale intervention. Laila's information was the missing piece of the puzzle.

The information exchange was brief, efficient, yet heavy with the gravity of the situation. Time was of the essence. The clock was relentlessly ticking down. Every second felt like an eternity. Laila hung up the phone, the silent hum of the rural landscape suddenly feeling amplified, almost deafening in its stillness. The weight of responsibility settled heavily upon her. This wasn't just about bringing down a terrorist cell; it was about preventing a national tragedy. It was a fight against time, a race against the very fabric of her own existence.

Her mind raced, processing the implications of her findings. She needed to act swiftly, decisively. She had to formulate a plan, a strategy to disrupt the terrorists' operation before they could strike. She began meticulously constructing a plan, outlining every detail, every contingency, anticipating every possible move the Serpent's Fang might make. She considered various scenarios, drawing upon her years of military and law enforcement experience, envisioning the layout of the ceremony, identifying potential security vulnerabilities, and anticipating the terrorists' likely approach.

Her tiny farmhouse was once again transformed into a strategic command center. Maps, photographs, intelligence reports, and detailed sketches of the National Remembrance Day ceremony venue littered the tables. Laila worked tirelessly, fueled by adrenaline and unwavering resolve.
Sleep was a luxury she could not afford. She was in a high- stakes game of cat and mouse, with the lives of countless innocents hanging in the balance. Her sharp mind raced, calculating

probabilities, analyzing risks, and devising countermeasures.

She knew the stakes were incredibly high. Failure was not an option. She had faced down death before, stared into the abyss of chaos and emerged victorious. But this was different. This was about preventing a national-scale disaster. This was about the lives of hundreds, perhaps thousands of innocent people. The weight of that responsibility was immense, almost unbearable, yet it fueled her determination. She would stop them. She had to.

The hours melted into a blur of activity. She meticulously mapped out the ceremony site, identifying potential entry points, escape routes, and blind spots. She analyzed the security measures in place, searching for vulnerabilities that the terrorists might exploit. She developed a multi-pronged strategy, incorporating elements of surprise, deception, and overwhelming force, ensuring she had a plan for every contingency.

Laila considered her own limited resources. She was a lone wolf, operating outside the traditional structures of law enforcement and intelligence. But she possessed unique skills and experience, honed by years of military training and law enforcement work. She was resourceful, adaptable, and relentlessly determined. She would use every tool at her disposal, every ounce of her experience and ingenuity, to thwart the terrorists' plan.

The impending disaster loomed large, casting a dark shadow over everything. But Laila refused to be intimidated. She was a soldier, a marshal, a woman forged in the fires of adversity. She was a force to be reckoned with, and she would not rest until the Serpent's Fang was neutralized, and the lives of countless innocents were saved. The ticking clock was her only true enemy, but Laila Aurora Wright was about to teach it the meaning of defeat. The hunt was on, and this time, she wouldn't just win; she would ensure that The Serpent's Fang would never slither again.

Assembling a Team

The weight of the impending catastrophe pressed down on Laila, a physical burden almost as heavy as the responsibility she carried. She couldn't do this alone. The Serpent's Fang was a sophisticated, well-organized group; taking them down required a team, a carefully chosen group of individuals with complementary skills and unwavering loyalty. But trust was a fragile commodity, especially in her line of work. Her past experiences had taught her the bitter lesson that even those closest to you could betray you. Her divorce from Frank, a man she once considered her confidante and partner, still stung, a constant reminder of broken trust and shattered expectations.

Her thoughts drifted to Robert Miller at the FBI. He was a seasoned agent, sharp and intuitive, but she knew his hands were tied by bureaucracy and procedure. He wouldn't have the freedom of action she needed. She needed someone who could operate outside the confines of official channels, someone who understood the shadows and could move with lethal efficiency. Someone like her.

The first person that came to mind was

Sergeant Javier Rodriguez, a former Delta Force operator she'd met during a joint training exercise in the Nevada desert several years ago. Javier was a ghost, a man of few words, but his actions spoke volumes. His expertise in close-quarters combat and demolitions was legendary, and his loyalty was unquestionable. He was currently working as a private security contractor, operating in the shadows, a perfect fit for the clandestine nature of this operation.

Reaching out to Javier was risky. He wasn't one for big operations or large teams. He preferred to operate alone, a solitary wolf like herself. But Laila knew that his skills were exactly what she needed to breach the security of the National Remembrance Day ceremony. A phone call was out of the question; Javier wouldn't answer to a simple call. She needed a more subtle approach. She decided to use a secure encrypted messaging system she had used before, sending him a coded message referring to a time and place they had last met - a desolate stretch of highway near the Arizona border, where they'd exchanged information during a previous mission. This was his language, and she was certain he would understand the urgency and the seriousness of her message.

Next, she needed someone with technological expertise, a digital ghost who could navigate the intricate maze of cyberspace and disrupt the Serpent's Fang's communications. Her mind went to Dr. Evelyn Reed, a brilliant computer scientist with a past as a National Security Agency cryptographer. Evelyn was fiercely independent, possessing an unparalleled understanding of cybersecurity and a knack for finding vulnerabilities where others saw only impenetrable walls. She was a recluse, preferring the company of her computers to people, but Laila knew she was capable of extraordinary things, a true digital warrior.

Contacting Evelyn was a different challenge altogether. She valued her privacy more than anything, and Laila doubted a direct approach would work. She decided to utilize a backchannel – an old friend, a retired NSA analyst who still maintained contact with Evelyn. This was a riskier move, relying on a chain of trust, but the potential reward outweighed the inherent danger. She needed to frame her request as a purely academic challenge, a complex puzzle for Evelyn's intellect to unravel. The stakes were high; failure wasn't an option.

Finally, Laila needed someone with inside knowledge of the law enforcement community, someone who could navigate the complexities of the National Remembrance Day ceremony without raising suspicion. She considered several options – former colleagues, confidential informants – but her thoughts finally settled on Detective Marcus Jones, a sharp and resourceful detective from the Philadelphia Police Department. Marcus had a keen eye for detail, an uncanny ability to read people, and a sense of intuition that often bordered on precognitive. He'd once been a part of her team during a case involving a stolen arsenal, and he understood her methods and her unwavering commitment to justice. She knew he wouldn't hesitate to help her, although he would also question why.

Assembling this team wasn't just about recruiting individuals with specific skills; it was about building trust, establishing a common goal, and forging a cohesive unit. It was about creating a synergy, a dynamic where the sum was greater than the parts. Laila knew that each member had their own quirks, their own methods, and their own reservations. Her leadership, in this case, wasn't about barking orders; it was about collaboration, about creating an environment where each person felt valued, understood, and respected. She had to convince them to trust her, to trust each other, and most importantly, to trust her instincts.

Reaching out to each of them required a

delicate balance of directness and subtlety, a calculated dance between authority and persuasion. She had to appeal to their sense of duty, their sense of justice, and most importantly, their understanding of the catastrophic consequences of failure. Each conversation was a high-stakes negotiation, a battle of wills and trust,

played out in the shadows, under the relentless ticking of the clock.

The challenges were significant. Javier's solitary nature, Evelyn's reclusiveness, and Marcus's cautious approach all presented unique obstacles. Laila's trust issues were compounded by her own past traumas, creating an emotional minefield that threatened to derail her carefully constructed plan. She had to overcome her own ingrained skepticism, her reluctance to fully confide in others, and her own deeply- seated fears of betrayal.

Days turned into sleepless nights as Laila juggled communication, coordination, and the relentless pressure of the approaching deadline. She meticulously planned the team's operation, anticipating every possible contingency, every potential roadblock. She had to ensure the team worked as a seamless unit, each member aware of their roles and responsibilities, their actions coordinated down to the smallest detail.

The assembling of this team wasn't merely a logistical exercise; it was a testament to Laila's leadership. Her ability to identify the right people, to persuade them to join her cause, and to forge a strong cohesive unit, despite the inherent risks and the pressure of time, demonstrated her exceptional skills as a leader. She had faced death before, felt the chill of betrayal in her heart; now, she was building trust, weaving a tapestry of collaboration from individuals who seemed incapable of trust. It was a dangerous game, a gamble with lives hanging in the balance. The ultimate success of this mission wouldn't just depend on their tactical prowess or strategic acumen, it would rest on the strength of the bonds she would forge within her hand-picked team. And Laila, despite her reluctance to trust, was determined to

make it work. The clock was ticking. The lives of countless innocents hung in the balance, and she had to succeed.

Race Against Time

The encrypted message to Javier arrived, a simple, almost cryptic, reference to a time and a place. He wouldn't need more. Laila knew he understood the gravity of the situation; the unspoken urgency hung heavy in the air, a palpable tension that only those who'd danced with death could comprehend. Days bled into nights, each hour a precious commodity in the escalating countdown. The Arizona desert highway, their designated rendezvous point, stretched endlessly under the unforgiving sun. The air shimmered with heat, mirroring the intensity of the situation. Javier arrived precisely on time, his presence as silent and lethal as a desert viper. No pleasantries were exchanged. The mission was laid out in stark, efficient terms – infiltrate the ceremony, neutralize the threat, and extract. Javier, a man of action, didn't need flowery explanations; he simply nodded, his eyes betraying the steely resolve that Laila had come to expect.
His departure was as swift and silent as his arrival, leaving Laila with the unsettling quiet of a successful, yet incredibly perilous, first step.

Evelyn Reed was a different challenge entirely. The backchannel – her old NSA friend, Thomas Ashton – was cautious, understandably so. Laila framed the request as an academic exercise, a complex cryptographic puzzle. She needed to hack into Serpent's Fang's encrypted communication system. The description was vague, the stakes implied rather than stated explicitly. Ashton, after a period of careful consideration, agreed to pass on the request, but stressed the importance of discretion. Evelyn, when approached with the "puzzle," reacted with her usual aloof detachment. But her sharp intellect recognized the challenge, the complexity, the almost impossible nature of

the task. The silence after she received the data was deafening, a testament to the intensity of her focus. Days later, a single line of code arrived – a key, a backdoor to the Serpent's Fang's communication network. It was a testament to Evelyn's brilliant mind, a digital key that would unlock the terrorists' plans. The risk was monumental – the slightest mistake could expose Evelyn, and the whole operation. But Evelyn, like Laila and Javier, was a calculated risk-taker.

Marcus Jones, the Philadelphia detective, was the final piece of the puzzle. Laila met him in a secluded corner of a diner, a safe house amidst the city's relentless energy. She laid out the situation, presenting him with verifiable facts— the intercepted communication, the identified suspects. Marcus, though skeptical at first, was familiar with Laila’s methods, and ultimately, her unparalleled success rate. The weight of his responsibility to protect and serve was tangible. He was willing to bend the rules, to operate outside of official channels, only if he could be certain of Laila's success. The threat level was clear; failure was not an option. He agreed to provide inside information – security protocols, personnel details, a layout of the National Remembrance Day ceremony venue. His meticulous attention to detail would prove vital in orchestrating the team's movements.

The clock continued its relentless march. The team was assembled, a collection of disparate individuals unified by a common purpose. Laila, drawing upon her experience leading a team in the Norwegian Forsvarets Special Kommando, established clear lines of communication, defined roles, and meticulously planned the operation down to the second. The complexity of the task was daunting; the potential for failure, catastrophic. Each member was briefed, their specific tasks explained, the potential risks laid bare.
There was no room for error, no time for hesitation.

The plan was intricate, a delicate ballet of timing and coordination. Javier, as the point man, would utilize his expert demolition skills to breach the security perimeter. Evelyn would simultaneously disrupt the terrorists' communication network, creating chaos and confusion. Marcus would utilize his intimate knowledge of the ceremony to guide the team, identifying potential threats and escape routes. Laila, the tactical mastermind, would oversee the entire operation, making split-second decisions, adapting to changing circumstances, always aware of the ever-present threat of failure.

The operation began under the cover of darkness, a cloak of secrecy shrouding their actions. Javier's explosive expertise disabled the perimeter security with surgical precision, creating a diversion that masked the team's movement.
Evelyn's digital prowess unleashed a cascade of malfunctions, throwing the terrorists' communication into disarray. Marcus, navigating the crowded corridors of the ceremony venue, guided the team through the maze-like layout, expertly avoiding security personnel. Laila, ever watchful, directed her team with sharp commands, anticipating the terrorists' moves, adapting to their unpredictable actions.

The confrontation was brutal, a violent clash of wills, a chaotic dance of death. The terrorists, expecting to meet a compliant audience, were unprepared for the highly trained, brutally efficient counterattack. Javier moved with lethal grace, neutralizing threats with calm precision. Laila's physical skills, often underestimated due to her small frame, proved to be a deadly advantage, her close-quarters combat skills disarming and incapacitating opponents with brutal efficiency. The battle raged, a maelstrom of gunfire and explosions, adrenaline pumping through veins, the air thick with the smell of gunpowder and fear.

The terrorists' meticulous plan, their elaborate plot, was unraveling before them. The meticulously coordinated attack was met with a precisely planned counteroffensive, each action a calculated response, each move a testament to Laila's strategic brilliance and the team's flawless execution. The terrorists, initially confident, were now overwhelmed, their meticulously laid plan crumbling around them.

The final moments were a blur of motion, a frantic scramble for survival. Laila, facing the lead terrorist, exchanged gunfire in a deadly standoff. In a swift, precise move, she disarmed him, ending the immediate threat. The remaining terrorists were swiftly neutralized.

The crisis was over.

The aftermath was a scene of controlled chaos. Emergency responders arrived, the wounded were treated, the scene secured. Laila, her face streaked with grime and sweat, stood amid the wreckage, a silent testament to her determination, her unwavering commitment to justice. The ticking clock had finally stopped. The lives of countless innocents had been saved. But the emotional toll of the ordeal was immense, a lingering weight of the near-miss catastrophe.

The victory was hard-won, bought with sweat, blood, and the shared risk of a dedicated team. The mission was successful, but the cost, though immeasurable, would linger long after the final gunshot had faded into the silent echoes of the night. The threat was neutralized, but the fight, Laila knew, was far from over. The Serpent's Fang had been dealt a devastating blow, but their reach, their influence, remained a dangerous, ever-present reality.

The Ambush

The celebratory air of the National Remembrance Day ceremony hung heavy, a stark contrast to the icy dread that gripped Laila. The carefully orchestrated plan, rehearsed countless times, felt fragile, vulnerable in the face of the unpredictable. They moved like phantoms through the meticulously planned routes, Marcus's insider knowledge proving invaluable as they navigated the labyrinthine corridors of the event hall. Javier, ever vigilant, maintained a tactical rearguard, his hand never far from his silenced pistol. Evelyn, a silent guardian angel in the digital realm, monitored the terrorists' communication, providing real-time updates through their encrypted channel.

Then, it happened.

A deafening roar ripped through the carefully constructed façade of normalcy. Explosions blossomed like macabre fireworks, shattering the illusion of security. Screams mingled with the staccato bursts of gunfire. Chaos erupted, a maelstrom of panicked civilians, fleeing officers, and the cold, calculated movements of the terrorists. The ambush, expertly timed and executed, caught them off guard, shattering the illusion of control.

Laila felt a sickening lurch in her stomach. This wasn't part of the plan. This was raw, brutal, unplanned chaos. The meticulously crafted strategy was thrown into disarray, forcing her to improvise, to react, to adapt in the face of overwhelming odds. The carefully coordinated ballet had descended into a brutal, desperate brawl.

The terrorists, clad in fake police uniforms, emerged from the shadows, their assault a carefully choreographed symphony of violence. They fired with brutal efficiency, aiming for maximum casualties, creating a scene of pandemonium designed to sow fear and panic. The element of surprise, so crucial to their strategy, had been turned against them.

Laila's training kicked in, overriding the initial shock. She reacted instinctively, her small frame a deceptive camouflage for the lethal predator within. She dove for cover behind a marble pillar, the impact jarring her, but her mind raced, assessing the situation, formulating a response. The screams of the terrified crowd were a deafening backdrop to the sharp crack of gunfire.

Her team, equally proficient, reacted with practiced precision. Javier, utilizing the chaos as cover, used his demolition skills to create diversions, drawing the enemy's attention away from the more vulnerable parts of the crowd. Evelyn, despite the interruptions to their communication network, managed to maintain a precarious connection, providing crucial intelligence updates – the terrorist positions, their numbers, their movements. Marcus, using his knowledge of the venue's layout, guided the team through the treacherous labyrinth, directing them towards less heavily guarded areas.

The close-quarters combat was brutal. Laila's years of training with the Forsvarets Special Kommando in Norway, honed during countless missions in unforgiving environments, provided a crucial edge. She moved with the fluid grace of a seasoned warrior, a lethal ballerina dancing amidst the chaos. Her small stature was an advantage, allowing her to slip through tight spaces, to take unexpected positions, making her an elusive and unpredictable target.

She engaged the terrorists in hand-to-hand combat, her movements precise, deadly, a blur of motion. Her strikes were swift, efficient, aimed at disabling her opponents rather than killing them – a calculated decision that minimized casualties and maximized the chances of capturing them alive. Her training with the Norwegian commandos had instilled in her a deep understanding of leverage points and pressure points – the ability to incapacitate opponents with minimal force, preserving their ability to provide intelligence.

Javier's demolition skills bought them precious seconds. Explosions echoed through the halls, drawing the attention of the terrorists. The carefully planned ambush was being met with equally precise countermeasures. Laila used the confusion to her advantage, moving stealthily, silently taking down her opponents, one by one. She moved from shadow to shadow, a ghost in the maelstrom, her movements precise and deadly.

The fight was a brutal, visceral experience – a close-quarters combat ballet of death and survival. The air filled with the acrid stench of gunpowder, the metallic tang of blood, and the raw, primal scream of adrenaline. The sounds of shattering glass, the screams of the wounded, the staccato bursts of gunfire formed a cacophony of terror that tested the resolve of even the most hardened warrior. Laila pressed on, her focus unwavering, her resolve absolute.

Evelyn's digital expertise also proved essential. She worked tirelessly, hacking into the terrorists' communication systems, jamming their signals, and planting false information to create further confusion among their ranks. Her skillful manipulation of the terrorists' own technology became a powerful weapon in their counter-offensive.

One by one, the terrorists fell. Their carefully orchestrated plan, once so promising, was crumbling into chaos. Laila’s team, despite the unexpected ambush, showed flawless execution of their individual roles. Their training, their camaraderie, their shared purpose pulled them through.

The final confrontation was a fierce, almost surreal standoff. The leader of the terrorist cell, a hulking figure with eyes filled with chilling rage, faced Laila. He was bigger, stronger, but Laila's expertise in close quarters combat gave her the edge. In a swift, decisive maneuver, she disarmed him, using his own weapon against him, incapacitating him with a precise strike to his carotid artery.

The remaining terrorists, seeing their leader subdued, surrendered, their carefully constructed facade of defiance crumbling. The ambush, initially a devastating blow, had been transformed into a resounding victory. The crisis was over, but the emotional toll was heavy.

The aftermath was a scene of controlled chaos.

Emergency responders swarmed the scene, tending to the wounded, comforting the terrified survivors. Laila, her body aching, her senses reeling, surveyed the scene. Her team stood beside her, exhausted, battered, but victorious. The operation had succeeded, but the cost, both physical and emotional, was immeasurable. The victory was hard-won, bought with sweat, blood, and the shared risk of a dedicated team. The fight, Laila knew, was far from over, but for now, the immediate threat had been neutralized. The Serpent's Fang had been dealt a crippling blow, but their shadow loomed large, a reminder that the war was far from won.

Hand to Hand Combat

The terrorist, a mountain of a man with a face contorted by rage, lunged at Laila. His fist, the size of a small watermelon, whistled through the air, aimed squarely at her jaw. Years of instinct took over. She didn't try to block; she anticipated, her body a coiled spring, ready to unleash a counter-attack. She ducked under the wild swing, the force of the blow causing a tremor through the floor. As he overextended, she exploited the opening, her foot shooting out, a lightning-fast kick to his knee joint. His weight shifted, his momentum broken, a grunt escaping his lips.

He roared, the sound guttural and animalistic, his anger fueling a renewed assault. But Laila was already in motion. She moved with a speed and precision honed over years of rigorous training, each movement fluid and deadly. Her training with the Forsvarets Special Kommando wasn't just about brute force; it was about efficiency, about using leverage and precision to neutralize an opponent with minimal effort. She used his own weight against him, her grip finding his bicep, twisting with the force of a vise. His howl of pain echoed through the ravaged hall. She followed the bicep manipulation with a sharp elbow strike to his solar plexus, driving the air from his lungs.

He doubled over, gasping for breath. Laila didn't hesitate, her movements a blur. A quick chop to the back of his neck sent him sprawling to the ground, unconscious but unharmed. The entire sequence, from the initial attack to his incapacitation, took mere seconds, a testament to her lethal efficiency. It wasn't a display of raw power, but of controlled precision, a calculated dance of death performed with ruthless grace.

Another terrorist, smaller but equally vicious, charged, brandishing a knife with a chilling gleam in his eyes. This was a different kind of threat – a more agile, unpredictable opponent. Laila met his attack with a combination of defensive maneuvers and swift counter-strikes. She used her small stature to her advantage, slipping under his reach, her footwork a whirlwind of controlled chaos. She parried his thrusts, deflecting his blade with her forearm, the impact jarring but not debilitating. She countered with a devastating kick to his groin, the sound muffled by the surrounding chaos.

He crumpled, clutching at himself, his attack completely neutralized. Laila didn’t waste time. She seized the opportunity, quickly disarming him, her movements precise, her grip relentless.

She controlled his movements, rendering him completely immobile before tossing the knife away.

The fight wasn't just about physical prowess; it was about mental acuity. Laila's ability to assess an opponent's strengths and weaknesses, to predict their movements, was as crucial as her physical capabilities. She had to think three steps ahead, to anticipate their intentions, to counter their maneuvers before they were even fully formed. This required intense focus, a finely honed sense of awareness, a mind that functioned as quickly as her body.

She moved through the chaos, a phantom in the midst of the storm, her senses heightened, her movements almost imperceptible. Each encounter was a study in controlled violence, her training taking over, eliminating threats with precision and efficiency. She avoided unnecessary bloodshed, focusing on disabling rather than killing, preserving the potential for intelligence gathering later. She knew that every captured terrorist was a potential source of

information, a key to understanding the broader scope of the conspiracy.

One terrorist, cornered and desperate, lunged at

her with a wild flurry of punches. Laila responded with a series of precise blocks and counterattacks. She utilized the Kravl technique, a close-quarters fighting method she'd mastered during her time with the Norwegian commandos. It was a brutal, effective style emphasizing control, leverage, and devastating strikes aimed at vulnerable points. She used her elbows and knees, exploiting the close confines of the space, maximizing her reach and power. The terrorist, unable to cope with her speed and precision, soon found himself overwhelmed and disoriented.

Another terrorist attempted a takedown, aiming for a chokehold. But Laila was ready. She anticipated the move, her body reacting before her conscious mind processed the threat. She countered with a swift hip throw, sending the terrorist crashing to the ground. She followed with a controlled strike to the temple, rendering him unconscious. It was a testament to her unwavering focus and her years of intense training.

Each encounter was a ballet of calculated violence, a brutal dance of survival. Laila moved with the fluid grace of a predator, her movements swift and precise, each strike carefully aimed, each counter-move perfectly timed. She fought not with blind rage, but with controlled fury, her mind sharp and focused, her senses hyper-alert. The chaos surrounding her was deafening, but she moved through it with an almost serene calm, her focus unwavering.

Her smaller stature, often underestimated, became her greatest advantage in these close-quarters battles. She could slip through tight spaces, move beneath the radar of larger, less agile opponents. She was a ghost in the whirlwind of violence, an elusive force that struck with brutal efficiency. Her opponents, often larger and stronger, were taken down with the speed and precision of a seasoned professional.

The close-quarters combat was brutal, exhausting. The air filled with the acrid smell of gunpowder, the metallic tang of blood, and the overwhelming stench of sweat and fear. Laila felt the sting of bruises, the dull ache of strained muscles, but her adrenaline surged, masking the pain, driving her onward. Each victory fueled her determination, reinforcing her belief that she could overcome the odds.

She moved with a relentless determination, her small frame a deceptive camouflage for the lethal warrior within. She was a force of nature, a whirlwind of controlled aggression, a testament to the power of disciplined training and unwavering resolve. Her skill wasn't just about physical prowess; it was about the sharp, analytical mind that guided her movements, the unwavering focus that allowed her to see through the chaos and find the precise opening for a decisive strike.

Laila fought not just for survival but for a higher purpose. She fought for the fallen officers, for the innocent civilians caught in the crossfire, for the sanctity of law and order. Her actions were a testament to her commitment, a reflection of her unwavering dedication to justice.

The final confrontation left her gasping for breath, her muscles screaming in protest, but the victory was sweet. The terrorists were subdued, their carefully planned attack thwarted, their violent intentions neutralized. The scene was a testament to her exceptional training, her innate skill, and her unyielding determination. The fight was over, but the battle, Laila knew, was far from won. The Serpent's Fang might be wounded, but they were still out there, their venomous strike still a lurking threat.

Tactical Maneuvers

The echoing silence following the last subdued terrorist was deceptive. The air, thick with the stench of sweat, blood, and gunpowder, still hummed with the residual energy of the brutal encounter. Laila leaned against a shattered pillar, her breath coming in ragged gasps, the adrenaline slowly receding, leaving behind the gnawing ache of exertion. She wasn't injured, not seriously, but every muscle screamed in protest. She checked her pulse; steady, albeit rapid.

Her team, Sergeant Miller and Officer Davis, emerged from the shadows, weapons still raised, eyes scanning the ravaged interior of the church. Miller, a seasoned veteran with a weathered face that spoke volumes of past battles, gave her a curt nod. "Clean sweep, ma'am. All accounted for."

Laila nodded, her gaze sweeping over the scene. The once- sacred space was now a battlefield, littered with broken pews, shattered stained glass, and the unconscious forms of the terrorists. The air hung heavy with the scent of death and destruction. But amidst the chaos, a chilling realization dawned upon her. This was just the beginning.

"Miller," Laila said, her voice low and strained, "secure the perimeter. Davis, start searching for any intel. Look for anything that can identify the group, their leader, their next target."

The meticulous search revealed a trove of information. Hidden compartments in the terrorists' vests held encrypted data cards and detailed maps, revealing a network stretching beyond Pennsylvania, implicating multiple cells across the country. The intricate plan, a meticulously designed operation, showcased a level of sophistication that sent a shiver down Laila's spine.

Their initial objective had been to disrupt the attack, neutralize the immediate threat. Now, the scope had expanded. This wasn't just a rogue cell; it was part of a larger, far more dangerous conspiracy. Laila knew that neutralizing these individuals was only the first step in a much larger and perilous game.

Laila's military background shone through as she orchestrated the subsequent response. Her strategic thinking, honed through years of rigorous training and real-world experience, became paramount. She didn't just fight; she strategized, anticipating, planning, and executing with ruthless efficiency.

The team meticulously documented the crime scene, gathering evidence with the precision of seasoned investigators. Fingerprints, DNA samples, ballistic evidence – every detail was painstakingly collected and preserved.
Laila knew that the success of bringing down this network hinged on the quality of the evidence they gathered. She oversaw the interrogation, deploying her training in psychological manipulation to extract information from the captured terrorists. Her ability to read body language, to sense deception, was invaluable, proving instrumental in uncovering the larger plot.

Her tactical prowess extended beyond the immediate battlefield. She recognized the importance of establishing communication lines, securing backup, and coordinating with local law enforcement. She utilized her knowledge of radio frequencies and encryption to establish secure communication channels. She briefed the local authorities,
providing them with critical intelligence, ensuring a coordinated response.

The ensuing investigation involved sophisticated surveillance techniques, utilizing drones for aerial reconnaissance and deploying hidden cameras to monitor suspected locations. Laila leveraged her experience in infiltration and surveillance, guiding the team with her knowledge of evasion tactics and counter-surveillance measures. They tracked the communication networks of the terrorist cell, uncovering coded messages and intricate financial transactions, providing them with the breadcrumbs to follow the broader conspiracy.

One crucial element of their success was Laila's understanding of the terrain. Her familiarity with the Pennsylvania landscape, coupled with her military training in navigation and reconnaissance, proved invaluable in tracking the terrorists' movements. She used satellite imagery, topographic maps, and her own intuitive understanding of the region to predict their escape routes and anticipate their actions.

The pursuit involved high-speed chases, stealth operations in dense forests, and perilous infiltration missions in abandoned buildings. Laila's agility and tactical skills proved to be an asset in each scenario. Her small stature allowed her to navigate tight spaces and escape the notice of her pursuers, providing her with the element of surprise. Her years of training in hand-to-hand combat were critical in neutralizing unexpected threats.

One such encounter took place in a deserted warehouse on the outskirts of town. The warehouse was dark, its interior a labyrinth of stacked crates and shadowed corners. Two terrorists, heavily armed, were using the warehouse as a staging area for their next operation. Laila, with Miller and Davis in support, employed a flanking maneuver. While Davis created a diversion, Miller and Laila stealthily approached the warehouse, taking advantage of the cover of darkness and the dilapidated structure.

They moved with the precision of seasoned operators, their movements fluid and coordinated. Laila utilized her training in close-quarters combat to neutralize the terrorists. Her approach prioritized incapacitation over killing, aiming for disabling strikes that would allow for quick capture and interrogation. The encounter was a testament to the team's coordinated efforts, a flawless execution of a tactical maneuver that resulted in the capture of the two terrorists without any casualties.

The next encounter was more challenging. They tracked the terrorists to a heavily fortified farmhouse, nestled deep within the

Pennsylvania countryside. The farmhouse was surrounded by a high fence, reinforced with barbed wire, and armed with sophisticated security systems. Laila, using her knowledge of tactical breaching techniques, orchestrated a carefully planned assault.

Laila's expertise in urban warfare and close quarters combat was vital. She employed a layered approach, using distraction tactics to breach the outer perimeter, followed by a coordinated assault on the main building. The team used flashbang grenades to disorient the terrorists, creating an opening for a swift and decisive takedown. The operation was swift and decisive, minimizing risk to her team and resulting in the capture of several high-ranking members of the Serpent's Fang.

Throughout the operation, Laila displayed her leadership skills, her ability to inspire and motivate her team under

pressure, her calm demeanor amidst chaos, her exceptional tactical judgment, and her unwavering dedication to justice. She understood the importance of teamwork, relying on the expertise and capabilities of her team members to overcome challenges.

Each encounter, each tactical maneuver, was a testament to Laila's exceptional skills, her rigorous training, and her unyielding determination. She didn't rely solely on brute force but on cunning strategy, precise execution, and a deep understanding of human behavior. She was not just a soldier; she was a strategist, a tactician, and a leader. The pursuit was a constant test of her physical and mental endurance, but her unwavering resolve pushed her forward, driving her closer to dismantling the conspiracy.

The final confrontation took place in a remote cabin high in the Appalachian Mountains. The leader of the Serpent's Fang, a shadowy figure known only as "Seraph," was holed up in the cabin, heavily armed and prepared for a final stand. This was the culmination of the investigation, the final showdown that would determine the fate of the conspiracy.
Laila, Miller, and Davis surrounded the cabin, prepared for a final, decisive battle. They moved cautiously, utilizing camouflage and stealth to gain a tactical advantage. The assault was a carefully orchestrated dance of precision and controlled aggression, a testament to Laila's tactical brilliance. The cabin fell, Seraph captured, the Serpent's Fang, for now, neutralized. But even in victory, the lingering taste of danger remained; the fight might be over, but the war, Laila knew, had just begun.

Casualties and Losses

The radio crackled, the static a jarring counterpoint to the chilling silence that had fallen over the Appalachian mountainside. The crisp mountain air, usually a source of solace, now carried the bitter scent of defeat. The final confrontation with Seraph, while victorious, had come at a steep price. The celebratory adrenaline had long since faded, replaced by a heavy, suffocating grief.

Davis, his face pale and drawn, lay slumped against a snow- dusted pine, his eyes closed, a single, crimson stain blossoming on his crisp uniform shirt. A ragged breath escaped his lips, a sound that was both heartbreaking and terrifying in its fragility. Miller knelt beside him, his large hands gently cradling Davis's head, his face a mask of grim determination. The medic, a young woman with tears streaking her grime-stained cheeks, was working frantically, but the prognosis was grim. A sniper's bullet, precise and deadly, had found its mark, piercing his side just below his protective vest.

Laila felt a cold fist clench around her heart. Davis, her friend, her colleague, her brother-in-arms, was fading. The weight of his potential loss pressed down on her, a physical burden as heavy as the snow that blanketed the ground. She fought back the rising tide of emotion, the familiar fight-or- flight response battling against the overwhelming sorrow threatening to engulf her. Years of training kicked in; she needed to remain calm, clear-headed. There were still things to do, lives to save, justice to serve. But a chilling premonition whispered in the back of her mind – the cost of this fight might be far greater than she had anticipated.

The silence was broken only by the medic's murmured instructions and the rhythmic rasp of Davis's shallow breathing. Miller looked up, his eyes meeting hers, and a silent acknowledgment passed between them; the unspoken understanding that they had failed to protect one of their own. The heavy weight of responsibility pressed down on Miller, the veteran's stoicism barely concealing his own grief. The battle was won, the terrorists were defeated, yet a profound sense of loss permeated the air, a bitter taste in the victory.

The hours that followed were a blur of frantic activity. The airlift arrived, its rotors a jarring intrusion on the desolate beauty of the mountain landscape. The medics worked tirelessly, their faces etched with concern, but the grim reality hung in the air like a suffocating shroud. They loaded Davis onto the helicopter, a stretcher bearing a silent testament to the brutal cost of their victory. The whirring blades cut through the stillness, the aircraft disappearing into the swirling snow, carrying with it a piece of Laila's heart.

Later, in the sterile environment of the hospital, the official reports arrived, confirming what Laila had already known in her gut: Officer Davis had succumbed to his injuries. The news hit her with the force of a physical blow, the weight of loss settling upon her shoulders, heavy and suffocating. The room spun, the sterile white walls blurring into a chaotic vortex of grief and regret.

The loss of Davis was more than just the death of a colleague; it was a betrayal of the implicit trust that formed the bedrock of their brotherhood-in-arms. The camaraderie, the shared experiences, the unspoken language of mutual respect and unwavering support – all shattered by the cold, hard reality of his death. She had faced death before, stared it in the eye countless times during her career, but this was different. This was personal. This was the loss of a friend, a comrade, a soul who understood the sacrifices demanded by their profession. The grief was a raw, visceral wound, a painful reminder of the human cost of their fight against evil.

The weight of responsibility for his death pressed down on her; a burden she would carry for the rest of her life. She replayed the events of the raid in her mind, analyzing every decision, every maneuver, searching for any mistake, any oversight that could have prevented the tragedy. The guilt was a relentless tormentor, a silent companion that haunted her waking moments and invaded her dreams.

The ensuing days were a blur of memorial services, condolences, and investigations. The official investigation focused on the circumstances of Davis's death, seeking to identify any failures in their procedures or tactics that could have contributed to the tragedy. Laila cooperated fully, recounting the events of the raid with chilling detail, her voice steady despite the tremor in her hands. She felt compelled to ensure that Davis's sacrifice was not in vain, that their efforts to bring down the Serpent's Fang would lead to meaningful change in preventing future tragedies.

Yet, the official investigation felt inadequate, a cold, distant process that could never truly capture the depth of her loss, the profound impact of Davis's death on her team, on the department, on the lives of those who knew and loved him. The cold, clinical language of official reports couldn't convey the profound sense of camaraderie, the shared experiences, the unbreakable bonds forged in the crucible of combat.

The investigation yielded improvements in tactical procedures, leading to the implementation of enhanced safety protocols and improved communication systems. Laila's input was invaluable, her military expertise shaping the changes made to minimize the risks faced by law enforcement officers in future operations. But the changes were a small consolation, a pale substitute for the gaping hole left in their team, in her heart.

The weight of their victory, tainted by their loss, settled heavily upon Laila's shoulders. The successful dismantling of the Serpent's Fang offered a fleeting sense of accomplishment, a momentary respite from the unrelenting grief. Yet, the victory felt hollow, a pyrrhic triumph achieved at an unimaginable cost. She looked at Miller, his eyes reflecting her own sorrow, and knew that they would carry this burden together, their bond forged in the fires of shared trauma, their commitment to justice fueled by the memory of their fallen comrade. The fight was over, but the war, both internal and external, continued; a silent battle against the ever-present specter of loss, and an unwavering dedication to prevent others from enduring the same devastating pain they had suffered. The memories of the fallen would forever serve as a reminder of the high price of justice and the profound and lasting impact of their loss. The echoes of gunfire and the whisper of loss remained, a haunting testament to the grim reality of their profession, a stark reminder that in the shadows of victory, lurked the pervasive sorrow of sacrifice.

The Chase

The battered police cruiser fishtailed, tires screaming in protest against the unforgiving asphalt. Rain lashed down, blurring the already indistinct landscape into a watercolor of grey and black. Inside, Laila gripped the steering wheel, knuckles white, her gaze fixed on the taillights of the escaping vehicle ahead. Miller, beside her, navigated with the precision of a seasoned map-reader, his voice calm and steady despite the chaos unfolding around them.

“They’re heading towards the interstate, Laila. We need to cut them off before they hit the highway.” His voice was low, clipped, devoid of any emotion save for focused determination. He was a master of control, even in the face of imminent danger.

The terrorists' vehicle, a seemingly innocuous sedan commandeered earlier from a victim, weaved erratically through the late-night traffic, its driver showing a reckless disregard for the other vehicles on the road. The sirens wailed, their piercing sound swallowed by the storm. Laila felt the familiar surge of adrenaline, the cold precision of her training overriding the raw fear that threatened to overwhelm her.

She had faced down heavily armed insurgents in the mountains of Norway, survived ambushes in the Iraqi desert, and engaged in close-quarters combat in the backstreets of Baghdad. Yet, this felt different. This was a race against time, a desperate gamble against a clock ticking down to a catastrophic event. She was not only chasing terrorists; she was chasing the ghosts of Davis, his sacrifice fueling her relentless pursuit.

The chase was a blur of flashing lights, screeching tires, and near misses. Laila expertly maneuvered the damaged cruiser through the congested streets, her movements instinctual, honed by years of rigorous training. She anticipated the terrorists' moves, reading their every swerve and sudden brake, reacting with an almost supernatural speed and accuracy. Each near-collision was a test of skill, a calculated risk in a deadly game of cat and mouse.

Miller, eyes glued to the city map spread across his lap, called out directions with a calm authority that belied the perilous situation. His voice was a lifeline, grounding Laila in the present, preventing her from being swallowed by the rising tide of emotion. He was the steady anchor amidst the storm.

The rain intensified, transforming the streets into treacherous rivers of water. Visibility was reduced to near zero, each turn a gamble, each maneuver a calculated risk. Laila fought against the blurring of her vision, focusing on the glowing red taillights ahead, her entire being fixated on the objective.

Suddenly, the terrorists' vehicle swerved sharply, taking a sudden turn onto a narrow, deserted side street. Laila followed, the cruiser's tires spinning momentarily before regaining traction. The escape route was a desperate ploy, a gamble on a less trafficked area.

The street was lined with dilapidated warehouses, their shadowed corners promising ambush and concealing danger. The pursuit had shifted from a high-speed chase to a deadly game of hide-and-seek, the odds shifting in favor of the terrorists. The claustrophobic confines of the narrow street amplified the tension, turning the relentless rain into a deafening roar.

Laila slowed the cruiser, her senses heightened, every fiber of her being alert to any sign of danger. The silence that followed was heavier than the rain, more oppressive than the shadowed walls closing in around them. This was close quarters combat, a battle of wits and skill, where a single mistake could be fatal.

Suddenly, a figure emerged from the darkness, silhouetted against the faint light from a distant street lamp. He was armed, his movements swift and deadly, and he opened fire. Bullets ricocheted off the cruiser's armor, the sound deafening in the confined space. Laila reacted instantly, the cruiser swerving to avoid the hail of bullets while Miller returned fire, his shots precise and deadly.

The exchange was brief, brutal, and intense. A tense standoff followed, a silent battle of wills played out in the shadows.
Laila held her breath, her senses on high alert, ready to react to any movement. The sounds of the rain mixed with the tension, blurring the line between environmental noise and the enemy.

Miller's calm voice broke the silence. "They're in the warehouse, Laila. Three of them. I've got a visual."

This was it. The culmination of the relentless pursuit. The moment of truth. Laila switched off the lights, effectively blending into the darkness. The cruiser's engine remained running, creating a gentle hum that could lull the enemy into a false sense of security. The silence was punctuated only by the rhythmic drumming of the rain and the shallow breaths of the tense officers.

She and Miller exchanged a look, a silent communication that spanned years of shared experience and mutual trust.

The plan was simple yet deadly: a coordinated assault, exploiting the element of surprise. They would hit hard and fast, leaving no survivors.

Their entry into the warehouse was as silent as death. They moved like shadows, their movements fluid, precise, and lethal. They were not just soldiers; they were ghosts, specters of vengeance silently stalking their prey. The warehouse's interior was a labyrinth of stacked boxes and forgotten machinery, an ideal setting for an ambush.

The terrorists were caught off guard. Their initial surprise quickly gave way to desperate resistance, but they were no match for the combined might of Laila and Miller. The fight was short, brutal, and decisive. The echoes of gunfire were quickly swallowed by the vastness of the warehouse and the relentless drumming of the rain.

The silence that followed was profound, heavier than the relentless downpour. The air hung thick with the scent of gunpowder and fear. The battle was won, but the cost, like the rain, was relentless. They had stopped the attack, but the shadows of loss remained, the burden of their fallen comrade a heavy cloak upon their shoulders. The victory felt incomplete, a harsh reminder that the war within, against grief and the ever-present specter of their profession's inherent dangers, would continue long after the guns fell silent. The chase was over, but their fight had only just begun. The battle had been won but at what cost? The question lingered in the chilling silence, more potent than the echoes of the gunfire and far heavier than the unrelenting rain. The hunt was over, but the war continued.

Analyzing the Situation

The warehouse was silent except for the drip, drip, drip of water from a leaky roof and the ragged breaths of Laila and Miller. The air hung thick with the metallic tang of blood and the acrid bite of gunpowder. Three bodies lay sprawled amidst the scattered debris, starkly illuminated by the weak beam of Miller's flashlight. Their faces were grim masks of disbelief, their lifeless eyes staring blankly at the indifferent concrete floor. The rain outside continued its relentless assault, drumming a mournful rhythm against the corrugated iron walls.

Laila knelt beside the nearest body, her gloved hand resting lightly on the cold, still chest. She felt no triumph, no satisfaction. Only a hollow ache in her gut, a familiar emptiness that echoed the loss of Officer Davis. The adrenaline had receded, leaving behind a chilling emptiness that settled deep in her bones. This wasn't the glorious victory the training manuals promised. This was brutal reality, the cold, hard truth of her chosen profession.

Miller checked the bodies, meticulously documenting the scene. His movements were precise, methodical, his face a stoic mask that betrayed nothing of his inner turmoil. Years of experience had taught him to compartmentalize, to separate the emotion from the task at hand. Yet, even his disciplined facade couldn't completely mask the grimness etched into his features.

"Three down," Miller reported, his voice low and even. "No survivors. They were armed with standard issue pistols and improvised explosive devices." He pointed to a crude device,
partially disassembled, nestled amongst the scattered weaponry. "Fortunately, they didn't manage to detonate any."

Laila nodded, her gaze fixed on the lifeless form beneath her hand. The initial surge of adrenaline had given way to a chilling clarity. They had stopped the immediate threat, but the larger picture remained disturbingly unclear. The attack, the sheer audacity of their plan, it spoke of a larger, more sinister network operating in the shadows. This wasn't just a lone wolf operation; it was a coordinated effort, a well- planned assault on law enforcement.

"We need to secure the scene and contact dispatch," Laila said, her voice devoid of emotion. She pulled out her radio, the static crackle a jarring counterpoint to the oppressive silence of the warehouse. The dispatcher's voice, distant and yet somehow comforting, crackled through the comms, a lifeline in the wake of violence.

As the backup units arrived, sirens wailing through the storm, Laila began to piece together the fragments of information gathered during the chase and the subsequent firefight. The meticulously planned ambush at the funeral, the commandeered police cruiser, the improvised explosives
—it all pointed to a level of organization and sophistication far beyond the capabilities of a small, independent group.
This was the work of a well-funded, highly trained terrorist cell.

The initial shock gave way to a meticulous analysis of the situation. She reviewed the details, focusing on the terrorists' movements, their escape route, their weaponry, and their communication methods. She recalled the erratic driving, the desperate gamble of using a side street, the crude but effective IEDs. Every detail was a clue, a piece of the larger puzzle. Her sharp mind, honed by years of military training and experience, dissected the situation, stripping away the chaos to reveal the underlying structure and intent of the perpetrators.

The analysis pointed towards a deeper conspiracy, a web of connections that extended beyond the immediate perpetrators. The precision of their plan, their knowledge of police procedures, and their access to weapons and explosives suggested inside help, a mole within the law enforcement community, feeding them information and facilitating their operations. The possibility chilled her to the bone.

"Miller, I need you to run a trace on the recovered communications equipment," Laila instructed, her voice firm, despite the tremor that ran through her. "Let's see if we can identify their contacts, their network."

The subsequent investigation revealed a disturbing pattern of communication interceptions and coded messages that pointed to a larger network operating across several states.
The cell was connected to other extremist groups, their reach extending further than initially suspected. Laila felt the weight of responsibility bearing down on her, the

knowledge that stopping these three terrorists was merely the first step in dismantling a far larger and more dangerous organization.

As the morning dawned, painting the sky with hues of grey and orange, Laila stood overlooking the scene. The warehouse, now secured, stood as a stark reminder of the night's events. The rain had subsided, leaving behind a world glistening under the pale light of a new day. But the darkness remained, a deep-seated shadow cast by the insidious threat she had uncovered. She felt the familiar weight of her responsibilities, the burden of protecting the innocent, the unending battle against the forces of chaos and destruction.

She knew that this was not simply a hunt for terrorists; it was a war, a silent conflict waged in the shadows, a relentless pursuit of justice that demanded every ounce of her skill, determination, and unwavering commitment.

The scene was cleared, the evidence bagged and tagged. The bodies were removed, leaving behind only the lingering scent of gunpowder and the cold emptiness of a battle won, but a war far from over. The immediate threat was neutralized, but the implications of the night's events resonated far beyond the confines of that dilapidated warehouse. This was more than just a terrorist attack; it was a chilling glimpse into a network of insidious plots, a well- oiled machine of destruction operating under the guise of normality.

Laila knew that this was just the beginning. The hunt was far from over. She had dealt with the immediate threat, but the shadowy organization behind it remained at large. The investigation would be long and arduous, a relentless pursuit of elusive figures who operated in the darkness, cloaked in secrecy and anonymity. The victory tasted bitter, a poignant reminder of the price of freedom, the constant battle against the forces of darkness, and the endless struggle to maintain order in a world steeped in chaos. This was not simply a job; it was a calling, a life dedicated to the pursuit of justice, a relentless fight against the shadows. The rain had stopped, but the storm within Laila raged on, fueled by a grim determination to uncover the truth and bring the perpetrators to justice, no matter the cost. The victory was hard-won, but the war was far from over. The fight had just begun.

Seeking Reinforcements

The grim reality of the situation settled upon Laila as the initial adrenaline subsided. Neutralizing the immediate threat was a victory, but it was a pyrrhic one, a fleeting moment of respite in a much larger, more insidious war. Three dead terrorists, a warehouse littered with evidence, and the chilling realization that this was just the tip of a much larger iceberg. The meticulously planned attack, the commandeered police vehicle, the sophisticated IEDs—all pointed to a highly organized and well-funded terrorist cell operating with disturbing efficiency. This wasn't a ragtag group of extremists; this was a coordinated effort, a well-oiled machine of destruction.

The weight of the situation pressed down on her. She wasn't just a former Army Ranger and U.S. Marshal anymore; she was the linchpin, the point person in a rapidly escalating crisis. Her sharp mind, honed by years of military training and law enforcement experience, raced through possible scenarios, analyzing the data, seeking patterns, and building a cohesive strategy. She needed more resources, more manpower, and most importantly, she needed to connect the dots, to identify the puppet master pulling the strings of this deadly dance.

Her radio crackled to life, the dispatcher's voice a jarring contrast to the silence of the crime scene. "Marshal Wright, we've got multiple units responding to your location. What's your current status?"

"We've neutralized the immediate threat, dispatch," Laila replied, her voice calm despite the turmoil within. "Three suspects are deceased. However, this was a coordinated

attack, part of a larger network. I need reinforcements, and I need them fast."

The dispatcher's response was immediate, but it was laced with the bureaucratic caution that often stifled swift action. "Marshal Wright, we understand the urgency, but we need to follow procedure. We'll send in a forensics team, a SWAT unit, and…"

Laila cut him off sharply. "Dispatch, this isn't a routine robbery. This is a potential domestic terrorist cell planning a large-scale attack on law enforcement. The perpetrators had access to military-grade weaponry and sophisticated IEDs. We're talking about a network, not a small-time operation. I need a task force, not a handful of officers."

There was a moment of silence, the crackle of static the only sound that filled the air. Laila could almost feel the wheels turning, the protocols clashing with the urgent reality of the situation. She knew that she needed to bypass the bureaucratic red tape, to leverage her connections and experience to secure the necessary resources. This wasn't a game; lives were on the line.

She reached for her phone, the cool plastic a stark contrast to the icy grip of fear that threatened to consume her. She had to call in favors, to tap into her network of contacts within law enforcement and intelligence agencies. The names and numbers danced in her mind—former colleagues from the Army, seasoned FBI agents, and experienced intelligence analysts. She would need their expertise, their skills, their unwavering commitment to justice.

Her first call was to Agent Michael Davies, a seasoned FBI profiler she'd worked with during a previous investigation.

Davies answered on the second ring, his voice gruff but alert. "Laila? What's the situation?"

She briefly explained the warehouse incident,

emphasizing the larger conspiracy and the need for immediate assistance. Davies didn’t hesitate. "I'll get a team mobilized. We'll be there within the hour. And Laila, don't hold back. This is bigger than we think."

Next, she called Sergeant Miller, the meticulous and reliable officer who had been by her side throughout the night's events. "Miller," she instructed, "I need you to coordinate with the responding units. Secure the perimeter, document everything, and get the recovered communications equipment to the FBI lab ASAP. Davies is sending a team." Miller, though weary, responded with his usual stoic efficiency, his voice a reassuring anchor in the chaos.

Laila's next calls were more difficult. She had to navigate the labyrinthine corridors of bureaucratic approval, convincing skeptical officials of the gravity of the situation. She used her persuasive skills, her calm authority, and her unwavering conviction to push through the resistance. She laid out the evidence, painting a picture of a sophisticated terrorist network capable of inflicting devastating casualties. She emphasized the potential targets, the timeline, and the clear and present danger to law enforcement and the general public.

It wasn't easy. There were doubts, hesitations, and procedural roadblocks. But Laila, fueled by her years of experience and her unwavering commitment to justice, persisted. She didn't shy away from confrontation, she didn't compromise her principles, and she didn't back down. She pushed, she cajoled, and she ultimately convinced the right people to allocate the necessary resources.

Hours later, a coordinated task force assembled. SWAT teams, FBI agents, bomb disposal experts, forensic specialists—they arrived in a whirlwind of activity, their presence a stark contrast to the chilling silence that had previously hung over the warehouse. Laila, no longer a lone wolf, stood at the helm, directing the operation with her characteristic blend of precision and unwavering determination.

The scene was transformed. The chaos of the initial assault was replaced by an organized and efficient operation.

Evidence was meticulously collected, communication lines were secured, and intelligence gathered. Laila oversaw it all, her sharp mind dissecting the information, connecting the dots, and building a solid case against the terrorist network. She coordinated with the various teams, providing guidance, offering tactical expertise, and inspiring confidence. Her leadership was undeniable, her experience invaluable.

As the sun began to set, casting long shadows over the warehouse, Laila felt a sense of cautious optimism. The immediate threat was contained, the resources were in place, and the investigation was underway. The bureaucratic hurdles had been overcome; the reinforcements were secured, not just in the form of additional personnel, but in the form of a unified and determined team, ready to take on this formidable enemy. The war was far from over, but Laila, surrounded by her colleagues, knew that they were ready to face it. The fight had just begun, but she, and the team behind her, were more than prepared to answer the call. The long and arduous road ahead stretched before them, but for the first time since that fateful funeral, Laila felt a glimmer of hope, a feeling that this fight, this war, could be won.

Technological Advantage

The rhythmic thrum of the helicopter blades faded as Laila stepped onto the tarmac, the crisp night air a stark contrast to the stifling atmosphere of the warehouse. The adrenaline still coursed through her veins, a potent cocktail of exhaustion and exhilaration. The immediate danger had been neutralized, but the war was far from over. The meticulous planning, the sophisticated weaponry, the chilling efficiency of the terrorist cell – it all pointed to a level of organization that demanded a more sophisticated response. This wasn't a street brawl; this was a technological chess match, and Laila was determined to play to win.

Her first order of business was to delve into the digital detritus left behind by the terrorists. The recovered laptops, phones, and encrypted drives held the key to understanding the network's structure, their future plans, and ultimately, their identity. She needed to dissect their communication patterns, map their operational structure, and identify their leadership. This wasn't just about catching a few bad guys; this was about dismantling an entire network before they could inflict further carnage.

Agent Davies, his face etched with the exhaustion of a long night, arrived with a team of cyber specialists. His eyes, however, held a spark of admiration for Laila’s quick thinking and decisive action in the warehouse. "Marshal," he said, his voice low, "your call was a lifesaver. We're dealing with a highly sophisticated operation here. These guys weren't amateurs."

Laila nodded, already immersed in the task at hand. She directed the team to prioritize the decryption of the encrypted data, focusing on communication logs and financial transactions. She knew that the digital breadcrumbs would lead them to the heart of the network. She'd spent years working with the best in the business, honing her skills in cyber intelligence, and she was determined to use every ounce of her knowledge to expose this threat.

The cyber specialists, a team of brilliant but often eccentric individuals, set to work, their fingers dancing across keyboards with the speed and precision of concert pianists. The room buzzed with the low hum of servers, the rhythmic click-clack of keys, and the occasional frustrated mutter as they encountered particularly stubborn encryption protocols. Laila, however, remained calm and focused, her mind already mapping out the potential avenues of investigation.

Hours melted into a blur of complex code, cryptic messages, and intricate financial transactions. The team painstakingly pieced together the fragmented data, revealing a complex network of communication channels, encrypted messaging apps, and offshore accounts. The terrorists used a variety of anonymization techniques, making tracing their movements incredibly difficult. But Laila, with her years of experience navigating similar situations, was already a step ahead.

She'd noticed a peculiar pattern in their communications—a recurring IP address that seemed to be the central hub of their network. This wasn't just a coincidence; it was a deliberate choice. Laila hypothesized that this IP address belonged to a server located somewhere in the dark web, acting as a central command post for the entire operation. Identifying this server was crucial; it would provide a window into the network's inner workings and potentially lead to the identification of the ringleader.

Using her extensive knowledge of various anonymization techniques and dark web protocols, Laila helped the cyber team trace the IP address to a server farm located in a remote region of Eastern Europe. It wasn't a simple matter of simply raiding the server; the process required finesse, strategic planning and patience. They needed to gain access to the server without alerting the terrorists and compromising the ongoing investigation.

Laila's former colleagues in the Forsvarets Special Kommando proved invaluable in this aspect of the investigation. Her network of contacts, cultivated over years of working in various international operations, yielded access to a highly specialized team of cyber warriors, skilled in covert operations and remote hacking. They deployed a series of sophisticated tools and techniques, carefully navigating the labyrinthine layers of security surrounding the server farm.

The team worked tirelessly, employing a combination of social engineering, network penetration, and advanced hacking techniques to bypass the server's security protocols. The process was like a high-stakes game of digital chess, requiring strategic planning, patience, and nerves of steel.

One wrong move could compromise the entire

operation.

Finally, after days of relentless effort, they breached the server's defenses and gained access to its contents. The information that cascaded from the server was overwhelming – a treasure trove of encrypted communications, detailed operational plans, financial records, and the identities of the key players involved in the terrorist plot. The scale of the conspiracy was far greater than they'd initially anticipated. The server revealed plans for multiple attacks targeting not just law enforcement, but also major political figures and critical infrastructure. The implications were staggering.

The data also revealed the identities of the key players. The ringleader, a shadowy figure known only as "The Architect", was a former military intelligence officer with deep connections in the criminal underworld. He was highly skilled, well-funded, and had a network of loyal followers willing to carry out his deadly commands. His tactical acumen and understanding of technological tools were evident in his strategies; he knew precisely how to use technology to conceal his identity, communicate securely and execute his plans with near-perfect precision.

Laila, along with Agent Davies and her team,

meticulously sifted through the data, constructing a detailed profile of The Architect and his network. They identified his financial transactions, his communication patterns, and his potential locations. This digital trail, painstakingly pieced together, formed the backbone of their plan to dismantle the terrorist organization and bring its ringleader to justice. The technology they'd employed hadn't just provided them with intelligence; it had given them a strategic advantage, a way to level the playing field and confront this sophisticated foe. The battle was far from over, but with the arsenal of information at her disposal, Laila felt a surge of grim determination. The war had begun, but this time, she held the most powerful weapon in the fight: information, extracted through careful planning and technological prowess. The fight for justice was now a fight for technological supremacy, and Laila was ready for the challenge. The next phase of the operation was imminent.

Forming Alliances

The raw data, a digital mountain range of encrypted messages and financial transactions, had yielded its treasure: the identities and locations of The Architect's key operatives. But information, Laila knew, was only as good as its application. She needed to translate this digital intelligence into tangible action, and that meant forming alliances.
Unexpected alliances.

Her first call was to Elias Thorne, a grizzled former CIA operative, now a recluse living off the grid in the Appalachian Mountains. Elias was a ghost, a whisper in the intelligence community, known for his uncanny ability to extract information from the most hardened individuals. He was also known for his notoriously independent nature and his aversion to working with anyone, particularly government agencies. Laila knew convincing him would be a challenge, a delicate dance of persuasion and mutual respect.

"Elias," she began, her voice calm and measured, "We have a situation." She didn't need to elaborate. Elias was already familiar with her work, her reputation preceding her like a phantom echo. He'd heard whispers of the Marshal with the steel gaze and the even sharper wit, the one who could dismantle a terrorist cell with the grace of a ballerina and the ferocity of a cornered wolf.

"The Architect," Elias finally said, his voice raspy, laced with the undertones of years spent in the shadows. "Heard whispers about him. Nasty piece of work. What's the catch?"

Laila didn't mince words. She laid out the situation, the scale of the threat, the potential for catastrophic casualties. She didn't offer money, not directly. Instead, she offered something more valuable: information. Specifics about a shadowy organization involved in arms trafficking, a network Elias had been tracking for years, a lead he'd never been able to confirm. The details, pulled directly from The Architect's server, were enough to make Elias sit up and listen. It wasn't about money; it was about mutual benefit. A currency of shared purpose.

"I'll help," Elias agreed, his words precise and clipped. "But I work alone. No strings attached." The deal was sealed.

Next on her list was Anya Petrova, a former KGB agent, now operating independently as a freelance intelligence broker in Prague. Anya was lethal, resourceful, and fiercely independent, with a network of contacts spanning the globe. She knew the dark corners of Eastern Europe better than anyone. Her connections were indispensable in navigating the complex geopolitical landscape surrounding The Architect's server farm.

Laila approached Anya with a different tactic, a direct appeal to her professional pride. She laid out the intelligence they'd gathered, highlighting the intricate nature of The Architect's operation, and the sophistication of his security measures.
She presented it as a challenge, a puzzle demanding Anya's expertise. She didn't ask for her loyalty; she appealed to her competitive spirit.

"Think of it," Laila said, her voice a low purr, "as a chess match with the highest stakes imaginable. He's a formidable opponent, but I know you'll relish the challenge. This isn't just about stopping a terrorist; it's about outsmarting a master strategist."

Anya, known for her sharp intellect and even sharper wit, met Laila's gaze. She considered the challenge, the risk, the potential rewards. The glint in her eyes spoke volumes. She was in.

Laila’s final alliance was the most unexpected – with Frank, her estranged husband. The bitterness of their divorce still hung in the air, but the gravity of the situation transcended personal grievances. Frank, despite their tumultuous past, remained a brilliant strategist, his mind a maze of tactical maneuvers and contingency plans. He possessed an encyclopedic knowledge of military technology and a unique insight into The Architect's operational methods. Their past training in Norway, honed by the demanding Forsvarets Special Kommando, had created an undeniable synergy. The foundation of mutual understanding, of unspoken tactical comprehension, remained. The shared language of special forces.

Convincing Frank was a different challenge altogether. This time, Laila appealed not to his intellect but to his sense of duty, his buried patriotism. She didn't rehash their personal issues; instead, she painted a picture of the impending chaos, the potential loss of innocent lives. She reminded him of their shared past, their vows, the shared training that bound them – a silent contract of courage and selflessness. She spoke of the countless lives that depended on their combined skills.

"Frank," she said, her voice soft but firm, her eyes reflecting the seriousness of the moment, "This isn't about us. This is about them." She gestured towards the mountain of intelligence reports on her desk. "This is about saving lives. We can do this. Together."

He looked at her, his expression a mixture of reluctance and grudging respect. The wariness in his eyes didn't fully disappear, but a glimmer of determination replaced it. The shared history spoke louder than the hurt feelings. The shared language of military training filled the gap of their broken communication.

“Fine,” he conceded, a hint of defiance in his voice. “But I’m doing this for the country, not for you.” Their past lingered between them, yet the unspoken agreement resonated with the familiar weight of their shared training. Their combined skills, their specialized knowledge and intuitive understanding, had to form a bridge across their broken personal lives. Their alliance was forged not in trust but in necessity, a grim testament to the reality that some battles must be fought side-by-side, even if the personal war rages on.

With her unlikely allies secured, Laila felt a surge of confidence. She had assembled a team unlike any other: a ghost from the CIA, a phantom from the KGB, and her ex- husband, a ghost of her past. They were a force to be reckoned with, a unique blend of skills, experience, and sheer grit. The war was far from over; in fact, it was just beginning. But this time, Laila wasn't fighting alone. She had forged alliances, secured her strategic advantage, and was ready to confront The Architect and his network. The hunt had truly begun. The hunt for justice was underway, and it had now become a ballet of calculated moves, a battleground of wits and technological supremacy.

Preparing for the Final Confrontation

The Appalachian cabin, shrouded in the pre-dawn mist, served as a makeshift war room. Maps sprawled across the rough-hewn table, pinpointing the terrorist cell's planned route, their staging area, and their intended target – a heavily-populated section of downtown Philadelphia, near Independence Hall. Elias Thorne, his face etched with the map of a thousand covert operations, pointed a gnarled finger at a cluster of red pins.

"This is where they're going to hit," he rasped, his voice a gravelly whisper. "A coordinated attack, multiple entry points. Classic textbook stuff, but with a deadly twist."

Frank, his military precision evident in the way he held his coffee mug, leaned forward. "The twist being their use of a decommissioned police vehicle. They'll blend in, gain access, and then unleash hell."

Anya, sharp and elegant even in the rustic surroundings, tapped a fingernail against a laptop screen displaying satellite imagery of the target area. "Their communications are

encrypted, but I've managed to intercept snippets.
They're talking about a 'final act,' a symbolic strike aimed at destabilizing law enforcement."

Laila, at the head of the table, her gaze sharp and unwavering, surveyed her unlikely team. "We need to disrupt their communication, neutralize their advance, and apprehend them before they reach their target. We'll use a three-pronged approach."
Elias, a master of infiltration and interrogation, would infiltrate the terrorists' network, disabling their communications and gathering intel on their precise movements. His years of experience in covert operations would be invaluable in gaining access and extracting crucial information without alerting the enemy.

"I'll plant a virus in their system," Elias confirmed, his eyes gleaming with a predatory intensity. "Disrupt their comms, blind them, and give us an opening." He detailed a plan so meticulously crafted, so precisely engineered, that Laila felt a chill of professional admiration run down her spine. This wasn't just a plan; it was a work of art, born from decades of experience in the dark corners of the world. He would be their eyes and ears within the enemy's ranks, disrupting their operation from the inside.

Frank, with his military expertise, would lead a tactical diversion, drawing the terrorists' attention away from their main objective. He meticulously laid out his plan: a series of calculated actions designed to lure the enemy away from their main objective. This wouldn't be a frontal assault; it would be a chess match, a strategic dance of deception that would capitalize on the terrorist's own hubris and overconfidence.

"I'll set up a diversion, create a secondary target," Frank explained, his voice calm and controlled, betraying none of the intensity bubbling beneath the surface. "Draw their attention, create chaos. Give you and Anya the opportunity to strike." His plan involved utilizing specialized military tactics, designed to confuse and distract the terrorists, leading them away from their main goal and providing a crucial window of opportunity for Laila and Anya. Every move was carefully orchestrated, every detail anticipated.

Anya, with her extensive network of contacts, would provide crucial real-time intelligence and logistical support. Her connections would provide them with critical intel, allowing them to stay one step ahead of the terrorists. Her global network would be their eyes and ears, providing vital real- time intelligence, crucial logistics, and a critical lifeline during the operation.

"I'll keep an eye on their movements," Anya stated, her voice smooth as polished granite. "Any deviation from the plan, I'll alert you immediately. Think of me as your eyes in the sky." She outlined her intricate network of contacts, explaining how they would work in tandem to provide the team with a continuous flow of real-time intelligence. This network, spanning continents, would serve as their early warning system, enabling them to adapt and respond effectively to any unforeseen circumstances.

Laila, meanwhile, would lead the final assault, utilizing her exceptional combat skills and tactical expertise to neutralize the threat. Her strategy was a meticulously crafted dance of calculated risks and precision strikes, designed to neutralize the terrorist cell with minimal civilian casualties. She would rely on her years of training, honed by the harsh realities of military life, to coordinate the final assault.

"We move in three hours," Laila announced, her voice firm, leaving no room for doubt or hesitation. "Elias, you're in first. Frank, you're on diversion. Anya, I'll need your eyes and ears every second. And let's make sure this ends without unnecessary casualties."

The next few hours were a blur of activity. Elias meticulously prepared his digital arsenal, Frank meticulously checked his gear and mapped out his diversion routes, and Anya worked the phones, her sharp tongue and even sharper mind extracting every piece of information she could. Laila, meanwhile, ran through the tactical plan again and again, etching it into her mind, preparing for the imminent confrontation.

The plan was intricate, demanding perfect timing and flawless execution. One wrong move, one missed cue, and the entire operation could collapse. The weight of responsibility pressed down on Laila, but she pushed it aside. She had faced down far worse. She had trained for this, lived for this. This wasn't just about stopping a terrorist attack; it was about saving lives, protecting the innocent.

The tension in the cabin was palpable. The silence was broken only by the ticking of a grandfather clock, each tick marking the relentless march of time, counting down to the moment of truth. As the final hour approached, the air crackled with anticipation, a potent blend of fear and adrenaline. The team checked their equipment, whispered final instructions, and prepared for their roles in the unfolding drama.

Laila looked at her team, her unlikely allies, forged in the crucible of a shared purpose. She knew they were ready. They were a team of ghosts, phantoms, and broken hearts, united by a common mission – to stop a catastrophic attack and prevent bloodshed. Their shared experiences, their individual skills, and their unwavering resolve would be their weapons in the fight ahead. They were a force to be reckoned with.

As the first rays of dawn painted the sky, the team prepared to move. The battle for Philadelphia was about to begin. The final confrontation was imminent. The stakes were high, the risks immense, and the fate of countless lives hung in the balance. The time for preparation was over. The time for action had arrived.

The Siege

The pre-dawn light, a pale, sickly yellow, filtered through the grimy windows of the abandoned warehouse, illuminating the scene with a chilling, almost theatrical glow. Inside, the air hung thick with the smell of stale cigarettes, sweat, and fear. The terrorists, a motley crew of disillusioned souls and hardened criminals, were holed up in their makeshift fortress, unaware of the storm brewing outside.
Their chatter, a low, nervous hum, was punctuated by the occasional clang of metal as they checked and rechecked their weapons. Their confidence, once brimming, had ebbed, replaced by a gnawing unease. They sensed something was wrong, a premonition of impending doom hanging heavy in the air.

Elias, moving like a wraith, had already infiltrated their network. He'd planted his digital virus, crippling their communications, leaving them isolated and vulnerable. He'd managed to gather crucial intel on their precise movements, their strengths and weaknesses, their points of entry and exit. He was their silent observer, a ghost in the machine, providing Laila with the real-time updates she needed. The information relayed through Anya's network painted a vivid picture: the terrorists were preparing for their final, desperate act, a coordinated assault on Independence Hall, a symbolic strike aimed at the heart of American law enforcement.

Meanwhile, Frank’s diversion was unfolding flawlessly. His orchestrated chaos, a carefully calibrated blend of smoke and mirrors, had drawn the attention of several responding units away from the warehouse, buying Laila and her team precious time. Sirens wailed in the distance, a symphony of controlled pandemonium, drawing the terrorists’ focus away from their primary objective. Frank, a master tactician, was playing a dangerous game, but his expertise shone through as he expertly manipulated the situation to his advantage. Every move was a calculated risk, a step in a meticulously choreographed dance of deception, but the risk was justified.

Anya, her fingers flying across the keyboard, relayed crucial updates. Real-time surveillance footage showed the terrorists loading their weapons, preparing for their assault, their faces twisted in a grim determination. Anya’s intelligence network, a sprawling web of contacts across the country, provided a critical tactical advantage, giving Laila an unprecedented level of situational awareness. She kept a constant vigil, her eyes glued to the multiple screens, each displaying a different aspect of the ongoing operation. Every piece of information, every subtle shift in the terrorist's activity, was meticulously analyzed and relayed to Laila, giving her the precise knowledge she needed for a decisive strike.

Laila, positioned at the edge of the warehouse complex, her gaze fixed on the building, felt the adrenaline coursing through her veins. The weight of responsibility pressed down on her, but her training kicked in, overriding the fear. She surveyed the terrain, mentally mapping out her assault. The building was a concrete labyrinth, offering numerous chokepoints and hiding places, demanding a methodical, precise approach. She adjusted the equipment on her tactical vest: a Glock 17, a backup knife, high-capacity magazines, and a communication device that was constantly linked to Anya and Frank. Her heart pounded in her chest, a drumbeat of anticipation, fear, and excitement.

The assault began with a coordinated barrage of flashbang grenades, illuminating the interior and disorienting the terrorists. The sudden burst of blinding light and deafening

noise created an opportunity to breach the defenses. Laila led the charge, her movements swift and fluid, a symphony of precision and lethality. Her years of training in Norway's elite Forsvarets Special Kommando were evident in her every move, every precise step. She weaved through the warehouse, her movements a blur, taking down enemy after enemy with swift, precise movements. Her small stature belied her incredible strength and combat prowess.
Underestimating her was a fatal mistake many would learn.

Frank, having completed his diversion, arrived as reinforcements, providing covering fire and creating diversionary tactics while Laila systematically cleared each section of the warehouse. Their combined efforts turned the tide, and the chaos inside the building intensified, a deadly ballet of gunfire and close-quarters combat. The terrorists, disoriented and outnumbered, fought back with desperate ferocity, but they were no match for Laila's tactical expertise and Frank's military precision. Anya's constant updates provided critical support, ensuring that they were always one step ahead.

The siege was a brutal, claustrophobic fight, a deadly dance in the shadows. The sound of gunfire echoed through the warehouse, punctuated by the shattering of glass and the cries of the dying. The battle raged, a tempest of violence that tore through the warehouse's confines. Laila, moving with lethal efficiency, navigated the maze of obstacles, eliminating the terrorists one by one. Each enemy eliminated was another step closer to securing the safety of countless innocent lives.

The final showdown took place in the warehouse's central chamber. The remaining terrorists, huddled together, their eyes filled with fear and desperation, made a last stand. Their weapons, once symbols of power, now lay scattered

around them, testaments to their failure. Laila, her face grim, her determination unwavering, moved in for the kill, her movements a whirlwind of precise, lethal strikes. She disarmed and subdued them, securing the final victory.

As the dust settled and the last shots were fired, a wave of exhaustion washed over Laila. The warehouse stood silent, the echoes of battle slowly fading away. The threat was neutralized, the city saved. The weight of the responsibility lifted as she reflected on the operation's success. With the final terrorist subdued, the mission was accomplished.

Philadelphia was safe. The victory, however, came at a cost, a reminder of the brutality of the conflict and the sacrifices made to ensure the safety of the city. The battle was won, but the war against terrorism continued. The long road to justice still lay ahead.

Tactical Assault

The warehouse, a concrete tomb under the bruised twilight sky, pulsed with the ragged breaths of its occupants. Laila, crouched behind a stack of rusted barrels, felt the cold steel of her Glock 17 a reassuring weight against her thigh. Her breath hitched in her chest, a controlled rhythm against the escalating cacophony of the approaching assault team. She checked her comms; Anya's voice, calm and precise, filled her ear. "Team Alpha is in position. Team Bravo is securing the perimeter. Go when ready, Marshal."

Laila nodded, the motion barely perceptible. She adjusted the grip on her weapon, her finger hovering over the trigger. This wasn't a simple raid; this was a chess match played with lives. The terrorists, a dozen strong, were entrenched, their makeshift barricades a testament to their desperation. Their plan, a grotesque attempt to inflict mass casualties, had been thwarted, but their resolve remained. They knew the game was ending, but they were ready to take as many with them as possible.

The assault began not with a roar, but a whisper

– a series of precisely timed flashbangs that erupted in a deafening symphony of light and sound. The warehouse interior, momentarily blinded, was filled with the disorienting chaos of exploding light and concussive blasts. This was the opening gambit, designed not to kill, but to stun, to disorient, to create the crucial window of vulnerability.

Team Alpha, comprised of seasoned SWAT officers, surged forward, their movements honed by years of rigorous training. Their entry was a textbook maneuver, a coordinated ballet of lethal force. Simultaneously, Team Bravo, providing

covering fire from the perimeter, suppressed any potential counterattacks. Snipers, perched on rooftops, provided long- range support, neutralizing any threats emerging from the flanks. The entire operation was a symphony of perfectly orchestrated chaos.

Laila, her senses hyper-alert, moved with a predatory grace. She slipped past the initial blast radius, her body low to the ground, utilizing the cover of darkness and the disorientation of the enemy. Her movements, honed by years with the Forsvarets Special Kommando, were fluid and precise, each step calculated, each action a product of years of relentless training. Years spent in the unforgiving landscapes of Norway, honing her skills to razor sharpness, had prepared her for this precise moment.

She navigated the warehouse with the practiced ease of a phantom. The labyrinthine interior, a network of shadowed corridors and stacked crates, offered both cover and challenge. Her Glock barked, the sharp crack punctuating the air. Each shot precise, each round finding its mark with deadly accuracy. The terrorists, their initial shock fading, fought back with fierce desperation, but they were met with a wave of overwhelming force.

Frank, having skillfully orchestrated the diversion that lured away responding units, now arrived as reinforcement. His military precision was a stark contrast to the chaotic scene unfolding within the warehouse. His presence, a silent reassurance, bolstered the team's resolve. He moved with a measured intensity, systematically clearing sections of the warehouse, his weapon a constant extension of his will.

Their combined efforts, a deadly blend of military precision and marshal's resourcefulness, overwhelmed the terrorists' resistance.

Anya's voice, a steady, calming presence amidst the chaos, continued to guide them, relaying vital intelligence gleaned from real-time surveillance footage. She acted as their eyes and ears, monitoring the situation from afar, providing essential information about the enemy's movements and positions. Her constant updates were critical, turning potential ambushes into opportunities for decisive counter- attacks. Her technological expertise proved to be a deciding factor in their successful maneuver.

The warehouse became a crucible of intense combat. Gunfire echoed through the structure, the metallic clang of gunfire a stark symphony of destruction. The air filled with the acrid smell of gunpowder, punctuated by the shattering of glass and the groans of the dying. The engagement was brutal, claustrophobic, a deadly dance of precision and instinct.
Every corner held a potential ambush, every shadow concealed a lurking threat.

Laila fought with the relentless efficiency of a well-oiled machine. Her small stature, often underestimated, belied her incredible strength and combat expertise. Each encounter was a swift, decisive strike, a testament to her honed skills. She moved through the warehouse with a lethal grace, a whirlwind of precise movements, leaving a trail of incapacitated terrorists in her wake. Her training, her experience, her unwavering determination, all converged into a lethal force.

One by one, the terrorists fell, their initial bravado replaced by a desperate, futile resistance. Their weapons, tools of destruction and terror, were turned against them, becoming the instruments of their own downfall. The fight raged on, a relentless struggle for dominance, a battle played out in the shadows of the decaying warehouse.

The final confrontation unfolded in the warehouse's central chamber. The remaining terrorists, their faces contorted with fear and desperation, made a last stand, their weapons trained on the approaching team. But they were exhausted, outnumbered, and outmatched. Their final stand was merely a desperate, futile attempt to delay the inevitable.

Laila, her face set in grim determination, led the final charge. She moved with the speed and grace of a predator, her weapon spitting death with every shot. Her movements were a whirlwind of deadly precision, each action calculated to maximize efficiency and minimize risk. Her team, equally skilled and resolute, moved in perfect coordination, a well-rehearsed symphony of deadly precision. The remaining terrorists were subdued swiftly, their threat neutralized.

Silence descended upon the warehouse, a heavy, pregnant silence that followed the storm of the battle. The air, once thick with tension and violence, was now filled with the lingering smell of gunpowder and the metallic tang of blood. The echoes of gunfire slowly faded, swallowed by the vastness of the empty space. The victory was hard-won, a testament to the meticulous planning and execution of the assault.

Laila stood amidst the wreckage, her body aching, her breath ragged. She felt the profound weight of responsibility that had been lifted from her shoulders. Philadelphia was safe. Countless lives had been spared. The mission was a success. But the cost of victory was etched into the very fabric of the scene before her, a grim reminder of the violence that still haunted her reality. The battle had been won, but the war, the relentless war against terrorism, would continue. And Laila, with her hardened resolve and relentless spirit, would continue to fight.

Unexpected Twists

The warehouse fell silent, the echoes of the gunfight fading into the oppressive stillness. But the victory felt hollow, a fragile thing built on a foundation of shattered concrete and the ghosts of near misses. Laila, leaning against a toppled crate, felt the tremor in her hands, the lingering adrenaline a bitter aftertaste. The initial sweep had been textbook, but the unexpected had arrived with the chilling ring of a cell phone.

It was Anya, her voice tight with urgency. "Marshal, we have a problem. The secondary bomb – the one we didn't find – it's been activated. It's not in the warehouse, it's downtown, near City Hall. Estimated detonation: twenty minutes."

The blood drained from Laila's face. Twenty minutes. That was barely enough time to get to City Hall, let alone disarm a bomb planted by a group that had proven itself both resourceful and ruthless. Frank, his face grim, approached her, his eyes mirroring her own dawning horror. "We have to get there, now," he said, his voice devoid of its usual calm assurance. He knew this wasn't just another mission; this was a race against time. A race against annihilation.

The adrenaline surged again, a frantic, chaotic energy. There was no time for a coordinated assault; only a desperate dash against the clock. Anya, miraculously, already had a plan, feeding coordinates through their comms, directing them towards a rarely used service tunnel beneath the city streets. It was a gamble, a dangerous shortcut, but it was their only hope.

The tunnel was a claustrophobic labyrinth, cold, damp, and reeking of stale air and forgotten history. The flickering lights cast long, dancing shadows, turning every corner into a potential ambush. Laila, leading the way, navigated the darkness with an instinct honed by years of navigating treacherous terrain. Frank, close behind, provided covering fire, his weapon always at the ready. The urgency was palpable, every drip of water, every echoing footstep emphasizing the ticking clock.

Emerging from the tunnel, they found themselves in the heart of the city, a stark contrast to the grim underworld they had just escaped. The hustle and bustle of the city, usually a source of energy, now felt like a suffocating wave. Every siren, every car horn, was a painful reminder of the innocent lives hanging in the balance. Anya's voice, precise and unwavering, directed them through the teeming streets, her GPS navigating them through the labyrinthine city layout.

They arrived at City Hall, the imposing structure looming over them, a symbol of authority and stability under threat of imminent destruction. The bomb's location, according to Anya, was the basement, near the old archive storage. Anya had intercepted a text message during the warehouse raid that gave a clue to their plan. It seemed they intended to use the building's old storage facilities, now seldom visited, to conceal the bomb. The plan, however, was much more complicated than Laila had initially anticipated. The original plan was to have a bigger impact on the city. The terrorists were initially attempting to place the bomb near the main transport terminals. They had, however, stumbled across unexpected security protocols, forcing them to change their plans. It was in this scramble that they were thwarted.

They bypassed the panicked crowds, weaving through the throng of emergency personnel. Laila, in her civilian clothes, was practically invisible, blending seamlessly into the chaos, while Frank, with his muscular frame, drew less attention

than she'd expected. Their military training, their ability to adapt and overcome, was their only advantage.

The basement was a labyrinth of dusty shelves and forgotten records. The air was thick with the scent of mildew and decaying paper, a grim atmosphere that was only intensified by the looming threat of imminent explosion. The bomb, a crude but effective device, was nestled between stacks of ancient documents, its ticking a sinister metronome counting down the remaining seconds.

The bomb was a complex device, far beyond Laila's usual expertise. Disarming it was a risky proposition, a tense game of nerves against a ticking clock. But Laila had seen worse. She remembered the countless improvised explosive devices she'd encountered in her years in the army. She had dealt with bombs designed to inflict mass casualties, and although this bomb was seemingly a less powerful device, she did not take any risks.

With Frank's assistance, Laila carefully deactivated the bomb's firing mechanism. Her hands were steady, her mind clear, her movements precise. It was a race against time, a silent battle against the relentless ticking of the bomb's clock. Each wire, each connection, was a potential death sentence, but Laila moved with deadly grace and unwavering concentration. Her focus was unwavering.

With a final, satisfying click, the device was rendered inert. They stared at the bomb, the silence deafening after the tension of the preceding minutes. Their breath hitched in their chests; it was a victory bought with the cost of sheer determination and bravery. They had once again averted a catastrophe.

As the bomb squad arrived, sirens wailing in the distance, Laila and Frank exchanged a look. The relief was immense, but it was quickly replaced by a weary understanding. The battle was over, but the war against terrorism was far from won. The unexpected twists, the near misses, the sheer audacity of the terrorists' plans had left them shaken but not broken. They knew there would be other battles, other challenges to face. But for now, they had bought the city a reprieve, a fragile moment of peace in a world constantly teetering on the brink of chaos. The quiet victory, hard-won and deeply felt, was a testament to their skills, their resilience, and their unwavering dedication to justice. They had faced the unexpected, and they had prevailed. But they knew, deep in their hearts, that this was far from over. The fight would continue.

High Stakes Negotiations

The adrenaline rush subsided, replaced by a bone-deep weariness that settled in Laila’s limbs. Disarming the bomb had been a brutal ballet of precision and luck, but the threat hadn't vanished. The terrorists, whoever they were, were still out there, and the near-miss in City Hall was a stark reminder of their capabilities. Anya’s voice crackled through the comms, her usual crisp efficiency tinged with a strained note of concern. "Marshal, we have an active line. They’re demanding to speak with you.”

Laila's heart pounded against her ribs. A negotiation? She’d handled interrogations before, broken down hardened criminals, but this was different. This was a life-or-death gamble with the fate of an entire city hanging in the balance. She took a deep breath, steeling herself. This wasn't about brute force; this was about strategy, about understanding the enemy's motivations. “Patch me through,” she said, her voice calm despite the turmoil within.

The voice on the other end was distorted, a low growl that sent shivers down her spine.

“Marshal Wright,” the voice rasped, “we know who you are. We know your past. We know you’re good. Too good, perhaps.”

“I’m listening,” Laila replied, her voice even, controlled. She needed to buy time, to gather information, to understand their demands. “What do you want?”

“We want… assurances,” the voice continued, “assurances that the authorities won’t retaliate, that they won’t pursue us with their heavy-handed tactics. We want safe passage.”

Laila knew what they were doing. They were playing on the fear of the unknown, leveraging the very system she swore to protect. This wasn’t about a specific political agenda, Laila realized. This was about survival and the desperate measures people take when their back is against the wall.

"Safe passage where?" Laila asked, her voice neutral. She needed specifics. Vague demands were useless.

"Out of the country," the voice hissed. "We'll name our destination, and we expect cooperation. No SWAT teams, no FBI raids. A clean getaway. Fail to comply and we start activating the other devices."

The implication chilled her to the bone. Other devices. How many more bombs were out there? How much wider was their web of destruction? Laila had to tread carefully. She couldn't afford to provoke them. “I can't promise anything without authorization,” she responded, buying herself more time to work within the system. "But I can facilitate a dialogue. I can attempt to negotiate terms."

“We’re not interested in attempts, Marshal. We’re interested in guarantees. We have a list of demands that goes far beyond safe passage. These demands, if not met, will result in the deaths of hundreds, perhaps thousands. We are prepared to commit to these acts.”

Laila felt a knot tightening in her stomach. This wasn't a simple hostage situation; it was a full-blown terrorist plot, and she was the key negotiator. “Give me your demands. All of them. Let's discuss terms,” Laila said, her voice resolute, masking the fear that was now a cold fist clenching in her chest.

The voice on the other end relayed the list of demands: the immediate release of several political prisoners, a significant sum of money to be delivered to a specific offshore account, and a guarantee of non-prosecution for everyone involved.

The list was long, outrageous, and incredibly

dangerous. Each demand represented a critical breach of security protocols, a bending of the law that would send ripples through the entire justice system.

Laila knew the political implications of this were monumental. She could feel the weight of the situation, the repercussions of her decisions. She would have to play this extremely carefully. The wrong move, the slightest misstep, could send the entire city into chaos. This wasn't just about saving lives; it was about maintaining the fragile balance of power.

She engaged in a carefully worded back-and-forth, buying time to consult with Anya and other high-ranking officials. Anya, ever the resourceful strategist, fed her information from intercepted communications, giving her insights into the terrorists' mindset, their capabilities, and their ultimate goals. Laila used this information to her advantage, employing tactical concessions and careful negotiation to prevent further escalation.

The negotiations went on for hours, a grueling marathon of strategic maneuvering and psychological warfare. Laila, drawing on her years of experience in high-pressure situations, played the role of the sympathetic negotiator, the understanding party willing to listen. She didn't promise anything she couldn't deliver but managed to create a framework of hope for a solution.

However, the terrorists were cunning, each concession from her side drawing out further demands. It became a dance of careful concessions. It was a high-stakes poker game, with the lives of countless people as the stakes. Laila fought to control the conversation, employing her knowledge of human psychology, her uncanny ability to read body language and inflection, even through the distorted voice on the phone.

She pushed back against the most extreme demands, pointing out the futility of some of their requests, using logic and reason to erode their resolve. She painted a picture of a future where they could escape the consequences of their actions, where they might find a semblance of peace.

Meanwhile, in the background, law enforcement units were making subtle changes in their preparations. A covert team was assembled, preparing for a rescue operation if the negotiations failed, a plan carefully crafted to minimize civilian casualties. This was a back-up plan, a contingency plan should all else fail. Laila was buying time, hoping for a peaceful resolution.

As dawn broke, painting the sky in hues of orange and purple, the terrorists seemed to soften. Exhausted and possibly overwhelmed by Laila's calculated persistence, they agreed to a compromise. Their demands were significantly reduced, the initial threat of mass destruction replaced by a plan for a controlled surrender, with guarantees of fair trials and leniency for those who cooperated fully.

The agreement was fragile, a delicate balance of hope and fear. Laila knew that the aftermath would be complex, that the political fallout would be significant. But she had done what she could. She had averted a catastrophe, a devastating act of terrorism that would have shattered the city.

The relief was immense but fleeting, replaced by the weight of responsibility and the knowledge that the battle was far from over. But for now, the city was safe, a victory hard-fought and hard-earned in the crucible of high-stakes negotiation. The sun rose on a city spared, a testament to Laila's courage, her skills, and her unwavering dedication to justice. The silence following the tense negotiations was a fragile peace, a moment of respite before the next challenge emerged.

Neutralizing the Threat

The finality of the agreement hung heavy in the air, a fragile peace woven from threads of compromise and exhaustion.
The distorted voice on the other end of the line, once a venomous hiss, now held a weary tremor. They had agreed to surrender, to hand themselves over to the authorities, their demands scaled down to a level that, while still significant, offered a pathway towards a less catastrophic resolution. The initial threat of mass carnage had been averted, replaced by the less immediate, but still considerable, challenge of bringing these individuals to justice while mitigating the potential for further violence.

Laila felt the tension slowly drain from her body, the adrenaline fading to leave behind a profound weariness. Hours of intense negotiation had taken their toll, leaving her mentally and emotionally drained. She could feel the weight of the city, the weight of countless lives hanging in the balance, finally easing. The relief was palpable, a wave washing over her as the reality of averted disaster sunk in.

Yet, beneath the relief, a deep-seated unease lingered. This wasn't the end; it was merely a crucial turning point.

The voice on the other end finally went silent, the line cutting out with a final click. The silence that followed was deafening, the stark contrast to the hours of tense negotiation almost unbearable. Laila leaned back in her chair, her body aching, her mind still racing, replaying every word, every inflection, every subtle shift in tone. She'd played a dangerous game, walking a tightrope between appeasement and firmness, constantly assessing risk and calculating her next move. The success felt precarious, a testament to the balance she'd managed to strike.

Anya's voice broke the silence, her relief audible even through the comms. "Marshal, they're confirming the surrender. They've given coordinates, and we're deploying a team for apprehension."

"Good," Laila responded, her voice hoarse. "Make sure they're properly secured. No room for error." She knew the risks involved. These were dangerous individuals, capable of violence, and even with a surrender agreement, caution was paramount. The threat wasn't entirely neutralized; it was simply contained, waiting to be dealt with.

The next few hours were a blur of activity. Laila worked with Anya and the SWAT team, coordinating the apprehension of the terrorists. Every detail was scrutinized, every contingency planned for. The operation required meticulous coordination, a seamless blend of precision and force, balancing the need for a swift and efficient takedown with the imperative to minimize any further risks to civilian lives. The city held its breath, unaware of the delicate operation unfolding in its shadow.

The apprehension went smoothly, the terrorists seemingly subdued, their bravado replaced by a resigned acceptance. It was a stark reminder that even the most hardened criminals were capable of weariness, of admitting defeat. As the suspects were taken into custody, the city began to exhale, the collective tension releasing slowly, like the unwinding of a taut spring. The immediate threat had been neutralized, but the long process of legal proceedings and investigations still lay ahead.

The aftermath was as complex as Laila had anticipated. The interrogation process, meticulously planned and executed, yielded crucial information about the group's network, their funding, and the extent of their ambitions. The release of political prisoners, a core demand of the terrorists, was handled with extreme caution, each release carefully vetted to mitigate potential risks. The financial transactions, initially demanded as a ransom, were frozen, allowing for a detailed forensic audit of the accounts and the tracking down of the origin of the funds. The investigation was extensive, requiring weeks, even months, of painstaking work.

Laila spent countless hours reviewing evidence, interviewing witnesses, and coordinating with other agencies. Sleep became a luxury she rarely afforded herself, driven by a relentless determination to ensure the full extent of the terrorist network was exposed and dismantled. She worked tirelessly, fueled by a sense of responsibility and a profound understanding of the stakes involved. The city's safety, its sense of security, rested on the shoulders of her and her team.

Her relentless pursuit of justice extended beyond the immediate suspects. She delved deep into the web of connections, meticulously tracing the flow of funds, uncovering the layers of support, and identifying potential collaborators. She uncovered a complex network of individuals, a web of deceit that extended far beyond the initial group apprehended in the city. The investigation unearthed evidence of wider conspiracies, involving political figures, business leaders, and foreign entities. The implications were far-reaching, threatening to destabilize the political landscape.

The case became a national story, the details slowly unraveling in the media, generating public debate and political turmoil. Laila found herself at the center of the storm, her actions closely scrutinized, her integrity questioned. She navigated the intense media attention with a mixture of patience and steely resolve, steadfast in her commitment to uncovering the truth, no matter the cost. She understood the importance of transparency and accountability, ensuring every action was properly documented and justified.

Despite the pressure, Laila remained focused, her resolve strengthened by the knowledge that her work was making a difference. She continued to pursue the leads, relentlessly investigating the various connections, gradually building a case that would bring down the entire network. It was a long and arduous journey, filled with setbacks and challenges, but Laila persevered, her dedication unwavering. The victory was not immediate, not a single dramatic moment of resolution but a slow, steady accumulation of evidence, a meticulously constructed case that slowly dismantled the entire terrorist operation.

Eventually, the network was dismantled, its leaders apprehended, and its operations brought to a halt. The arrests, while not as dramatic as the initial confrontation, were equally significant, representing a comprehensive dismantling of a dangerous organization. Justice was served, not with a bang, but with the quiet but powerful impact of rigorous investigative work.

The aftermath left Laila changed. The experience had been grueling, emotionally and mentally draining, yet it had also strengthened her resolve and deepened her commitment to justice. She learned the importance of teamwork, the value of collaboration, and the power of perseverance. The experience reinforced her belief in the strength and resilience of the human spirit, the ability to overcome adversity and emerge stronger, wiser, and more determined. Though physically and mentally exhausted, Laila knew this wasn't her final battle. The fight for justice was ongoing, an unending struggle demanding constant vigilance. But for now, she allowed herself a moment of quiet reflection, a quiet acknowledgment of the victory, a hard-won success that had saved countless lives and protected the city from a devastating catastrophe. The quiet hum of the city, now safe and secure, was a testament to her dedication, a reward well- earned, yet a fragile peace that demanded continued vigilance. The battle was over, but the war for justice would continue.

Casualty Assessment

The silence of the city was deceptive. The streets, once choked with the frantic energy of a city teetering on the brink, were now eerily calm. But beneath the veneer of peace, a grim reality unfolded. The casualty assessment was a chilling reminder of the violence that had narrowly been averted. Three officers lay dead, their sacrifice a stark testament to the brutality of the terrorists' plans. Their faces, forever etched in the memory of their colleagues and loved ones, represented the price of freedom, a price paid in blood and sorrow. Anya, her face pale and drawn, delivered the news, her voice a low tremor against the backdrop of the city's hushed awakening. The weight of her words settled heavily on Laila's shoulders, an unwelcome addition to the fatigue already gnawing at her bones.

The injured were more numerous. Seven officers lay in hospital beds, their bodies battered, their spirits wounded. One was critical, clinging to life by a thread, his fate hanging in the balance. The images of their injuries – broken bones, lacerations, the haunting emptiness in their eyes – were seared into Laila's mind. She found herself haunted by the fragmented scenes: a flash of crimson against the grey concrete, a scream cut short, the sight of a fallen officer's lifeless eyes staring blankly at the indifferent sky. The sounds of sirens, the muffled cries of the injured, the grim determination in the faces of the paramedics – these were etched into her memory, indelible reminders of the violence that had come so close to consuming the city.

The damage to the city itself was less extensive than feared, thankfully. The terrorists' plan had been ambitious, potentially catastrophic, but their precise aims had been thwarted. The targeted area, primarily focusing on law enforcement, had seen significant damage – shattered windows, pockmarked buildings, vehicles reduced to twisted metal. Yet the scale of the destruction was significantly less than what could have been. Had the terrorists succeeded in their plot of deploying multiple explosives and weapons caches throughout the city, the aftermath would have been a scene of unimaginable chaos and carnage. The thought chilled her to the bone. This near miss didn't diminish the gravity of the situation, but it emphasized the potential for even greater loss.

The emotional toll was immeasurable. The

families of the fallen officers were plunged into grief, their lives forever altered by the senseless violence. Laila witnessed the raw, unfiltered pain etched on their faces, the silent tears, the choked sobs, the crushing weight of their loss. The image of their grief became another haunting memory, another scar etched into her psyche. She knew this was a wound that time would never fully heal, a constant reminder of the cost of the battle she had won. The weight of their loss settled heavily upon her shoulders, a burden that would follow her long after the dust had settled.

The next few days were a blur of formal reports, press conferences, and endless interviews. The city held its breath as Laila, now a national figure, recounted the events, carefully choosing her words, balancing the need for factual reporting with the delicate need to protect the emotional well-being of the victims and their families. The press, insatiable in their hunger for details, hounded her, their questions relentless, probing, often insensitive. But she held firm, her responses measured, her tone carefully controlled, her emotions tightly reined in. She understood the importance of communicating the truth, while simultaneously protecting the integrity of the ongoing investigations.

There were other casualties – less visible, but no less significant. The first responders, the paramedics, the firefighters, the police officers involved in the clean-up, all bore the invisible wounds of trauma. The sight of mangled bodies, the sounds of suffering, the sheer scale of destruction, had left an indelible mark on their psyches. The collective trauma within the department was palpable, a shared experience that would bond them, while simultaneously weighing heavy on their hearts and minds. Many would need long-term support, both psychological and physical, to recover from the psychological wounds that ran deeper than any physical injury. Laila recognized this silent suffering, the unspoken pain that lurked beneath the surface of their professional composure.

Laila spent hours visiting the injured officers, listening to their stories, offering words of comfort and support, acknowledging their bravery and sacrifice. Their stories, recounted in hushed tones, revealed the sheer terror they had faced, the stark moments of life and death, the enduring physical and emotional trauma. She saw their fear, their vulnerability, and their resilience in the face of adversity.

Their stories, raw and unflinching, were testament to the courage and fortitude of those who had stood their ground against overwhelming odds. Each conversation was a heavy weight, a testament to the consequences of violence.

The interrogation of the captured terrorists proved to be a slow, painstaking process. They were hardened individuals, accustomed to violence and deception. Their initial reluctance to cooperate slowly eroded, replaced by a weariness, a realization that their carefully constructed plan had crumbled, their hopes of chaos and destruction reduced to ashes. The information they divulged was fragmented, a mosaic of truths and lies, carefully pieced together by Laila and her team. It painted a grim picture, revealing the extent of the terrorists' network, their financial backers, and the sophisticated planning behind their attacks.

Yet, beyond the physical and psychological casualties, the aftermath revealed a profound impact on the city's spirit. The sense of security, once taken for granted, was shattered. Fear, once a distant threat, now loomed large in the collective consciousness. The city was healing, but the scars of the near catastrophe remained. The unspoken fears, the lingering anxieties, the constant vigilance, would cast a long shadow, even after the official investigations concluded and the media moved on to other stories. The city, once vibrant and confident, now bore the silent witness of trauma.

Laila recognized this collective trauma. She understood the city's vulnerability, its fragility in the face of such calculated violence. The near miss had served as a stark wake-up call, a reminder of the unseen dangers lurking beneath the surface of everyday life. The aftermath of the confrontation was not just about physical casualties or material damage. It was about the profound and lasting impact of violence on individuals, communities, and the very fabric of society. The city, once seemingly impenetrable, had been shown to be vulnerable, and the lingering fear cast a long shadow over its future. The battle might be over, but the war against fear and violence had only just begun. The memories, the scars, both visible and invisible, would remain, a constant reminder of the fragility of peace and the enduring strength of human resilience. And Laila knew, with a chilling certainty, that her work was far from over.

Investigation and Cleanup

The interrogation room was stark, the fluorescent lights buzzing a monotonous counterpoint to the rhythmic tick-tock of a clock on the wall. Across the table sat Omar, one of the captured terrorists, his eyes shadowed, his demeanor a mask of defiance that had begun to crack under the relentless pressure of the past few days. He was a ghost of the man who had so confidently driven the stolen police vehicle, a man who had envisioned a city engulfed in flames. Now, he was reduced to a broken husk, his bravado replaced by a weary acceptance of his fate.

Laila leaned forward, her gaze unwavering, her presence as sharp and honed as the blade of a scalpel. "The explosives," she said, her voice low and controlled, "Tell me about the explosives."

Omar flinched, his gaze darting away from hers. He shifted uncomfortably in his chair, the silence stretching taut between them, heavy with unspoken tension. He knew the game was over. His carefully constructed lies had crumbled under the weight of the evidence, the relentless questioning, the unwavering gaze of this woman who seemed to see right through him. The silence stretched, punctuated only by the rhythmic hum of the fluorescent lights, until finally, he spoke, his voice a barely audible rasp.

"There were five," he whispered, his words like shards of glass in the stillness of the room. "Five devices, strategically placed throughout the city. Each one powerful enough to level a city block." He paused, his breath catching in his throat. The details he revealed were chilling, painting a vivid picture of the destruction that had been so narrowly averted.

He spoke of hidden caches, of meticulously crafted detonators, of a network of accomplices who were now on the run. The information dripped from him, slow and painful, each confession a wound to his shattered pride.

The information Omar provided was crucial, a roadmap to dismantle the remaining elements of the terrorist network. The painstaking work of tracing the financial channels, identifying the collaborators, locating the remaining explosive devices – it was a complex jigsaw puzzle, each piece meticulously assembled by Laila and her team. They worked tirelessly, day and night, fueled by adrenaline and grim determination. The clock was ticking, every passing moment carrying the potential for further disaster.

The search for the remaining explosives was a race against time. Working in tandem with local law enforcement, Laila and her team meticulously scoured the city, following the trail Omar had laid out. Each location was a potential powder keg, fraught with danger. The tension was palpable, each step taken with careful deliberation, each breath held, as they searched for the silent, deadly devices. The sheer magnitude of the task was daunting, but Laila, ever the soldier, approached it with methodical precision, her military training kicking in, her eyes sharp, her senses alert, her mind a whirlwind of calculated strategies.

The discovery of the remaining explosives was a harrowing experience. Each device, carefully hidden in plain sight, was a stark reminder of the potential for devastation. The meticulous planning, the cold, calculated precision of the terrorists, sent chills down her spine. The successful neutralization of each device was a victory, but each success was hard-won, a testament to the courage and dedication of the team. The collective relief at the end was profound, a palpable wave washing over them, leaving a lingering exhaustion in its wake.

The cleanup operation was a massive undertaking. The city, while spared from the full extent of the planned destruction, still bore the scars of the near miss. The damaged vehicles were towed away, the shattered glass swept from the streets, the debris cleared from the affected buildings. The process was slow, methodical, a visual representation of the healing process. Laila observed the efforts, a quiet observer, her mind replaying the events, analyzing every detail, searching for ways to prevent a similar catastrophe from happening again.

The city began to breathe again. The streets, once deserted and haunted by the shadow of impending disaster, slowly filled with life, with the familiar hum of activity returning. The normalcy of life started trickling back. Yet, beneath the surface, the scars remained, invisible but deeply etched into the collective memory of the city. The wounds healed, but the memories persisted, a constant reminder of the fragility of peace and the ever-present threat of violence.

The media attention, initially frenzied, began to subside. Laila found a measure of solace in the quiet return to routine, but the experience had indelibly altered her perspective. She had seen the raw, unfiltered horror of violence, the devastation it wrought, not just on individuals but on the very fabric of society. The weight of responsibility remained heavy, a constant companion. She knew the threat of terrorism was not extinguished, but merely suppressed, a sleeping serpent waiting for the right moment to strike.

The formal reports were filed, the press conferences concluded, the investigations closed. The captured terrorists awaited trial, their fates sealed by their own actions. But the real work, the work of healing and rebuilding, had only just begun. The city needed time to recover, to reconcile itself with the stark reality of its near-death experience. And Laila, her body and mind exhausted, her spirit tempered by the fire of combat, began to plan for the future. The battle was over, but the war, the never-ending struggle against violence and fear, was far from concluded. She knew, with a chilling certainty, that her skills, her experience, her relentless determination would be needed again. The fight for peace was not a sprint, but a long, arduous marathon, and Laila Aurora Wright was prepared to run it for as long as it took.

The ghosts of the fallen officers, the echoes of

their silent screams, would forever serve as a grim reminder, fuel for her unwavering dedication to the cause of justice. The city slept, unaware of the silent vigil Laila kept, ever watchful, ever vigilant, forever prepared to face the unseen enemy, the shadow of terror that lurked just beyond the horizon. The aftermath had ended, but the reflection would continue, shaping her path forward, shaping the very fabric of her being. The fight continued.

Media Frenzy

The aftermath wasn't quiet. Far from it. The near- catastrophic terrorist attack, averted by a hair's breadth, had transformed Laila from a relatively unknown U.S. Marshal into a national heroine. Her image, captured in grainy security footage, then enhanced and broadcast relentlessly across every news channel, became a symbol of unwavering courage and sharp determination. The tiny, seemingly fragile woman, barely registering on the scale at 115 pounds, had single-handedly thwarted a plot that could have leveled several city blocks, killing hundreds, possibly thousands.
The media, ravenous and insatiable, descended upon her like a swarm of locusts.

The phone calls started before she even left the crime scene. Her small Pennsylvania farm, once a haven of quietude, was now besieged by reporters, cameramen, and satellite trucks. The driveway was choked with vehicles, their headlights illuminating her home like a stage. The peaceful countryside was transformed into a chaotic circus, a stark contrast to the tranquil life she had sought after her divorce.

Initially, she tried to ignore it, to retreat into the familiarity of her home. But the relentless onslaught proved too much. Every knock on the door, every flash of a camera, every insistent phone call, was a sharp reminder of the intensity of the situation. The normalcy she craved, the quiet solitude she needed to process the trauma she'd endured, was snatched away.

Her agency, mindful of the public interest and Laila's safety, assigned a public relations officer, a smooth-talking man named David, to manage the media onslaught. He set up a makeshift press office in her barn, a quaint and incongruous setting for the media frenzy taking place outside. David, a veteran of numerous high-profile cases, understood the delicate balance between cooperating with the media and protecting Laila's privacy.

The interviews were grueling. Each one was a careful dance, navigating the fine line between offering information to the public and shielding herself from the prying eyes of the media. She answered questions about her training, her experience, the specifics of the operation, all the while maintaining a calm and collected demeanor. But beneath the composed exterior, a storm raged. The memory of the near- miss, the palpable fear she'd felt, the weight of responsibility, and the exhaustion from the days of relentless work were constantly gnawing at her.

The media loved the narrative. The underdog story; the petite former soldier who took down a terrorist ring; the woman who saved the city. The headlines screamed her name: "Laila: The Angel of Megaverse City," "The 115-Pound Heroine," "The Woman Who Stopped a Massacre." She became an overnight sensation, a symbol of resilience and courage in a world increasingly consumed by fear.

However, the media's portrayal, while celebrating her heroism, often glossed over the emotional cost. The toll of her experiences—the sleeplessness, the nightmares, the constant replaying of the events in her mind—was rarely mentioned. The articles focused on her actions, her skills, her bravery, but seldom touched upon her vulnerability. This one-dimensional portrayal frustrated Laila, who desperately yearned for some semblance of normalcy and privacy.

There were attempts at deeper interviews, attempts to unearth the human beneath the hero. One journalist, a woman named Sarah from a national news publication, recognized the limitations of the "hero" narrative and tried to explore the emotional scars. Sarah listened attentively as Laila spoke about the fear, the responsibility, the haunting memories of the near-miss. She asked Laila about the personal cost, about her anxieties, her fears for the future. It was a humanizing interview, a welcome break from the relentless hero worship.

The interview with Sarah offered Laila a sliver of relief. It allowed her to express the emotional turmoil that had been swirling beneath the surface, to share the weight she carried, the burden she shouldered. It was a vulnerable moment, a display of humanity that resonated with the public, adding another layer of complexity to the "hero" narrative.

But the media frenzy didn't abate. The public demanded more, craved more details, hungered for more of her story. The attention, while initially flattering, quickly became overwhelming. Laila, accustomed to the quiet discipline of military life, found the constant scrutiny suffocating. She began to retreat further, limiting her public appearances, refusing interviews, shielding herself from the relentless glare of the media spotlight.

The constant pressure took its toll. The relentless glare of the cameras, the probing questions, the sheer volume of attention, began to wear her down. Sleep became elusive, her dreams haunted by the violence she had witnessed. She found herself increasingly isolated, her once-close friends and family unable to penetrate the wall she had built around herself.

One evening, after a particularly grueling day of media appearances, Laila found herself alone on her farm, the silence of the countryside offering a stark contrast to the incessant buzz of the media circus that had surrounded her for weeks. She sat on her porch swing, watching the sun dip below the horizon, painting the sky in hues of orange and purple. The serenity of the moment offered a momentary respite from the chaos of her life, a chance to reflect on the past few weeks, on the overwhelming events that had transformed her life. She felt the weight of the world on her shoulders, the burden of responsibility for the city she had saved. But she also felt a quiet sense of accomplishment, a deep satisfaction of having done what she had to do.

The media frenzy eventually subsided, replaced by the quiet hum of normalcy. But the experience left an indelible mark on Laila. The attention, the recognition, the praise—it was all fleeting, temporary. The true measure of her actions, she realized, lay not in the headlines or the awards, but in the quiet moments of reflection, in the deep-seated knowledge that she had prevented a tragedy, that she had protected innocent lives. The scars remained, both visible and invisible, a constant reminder of the price of courage, and the resilience of the human spirit. The city was healing, and so was she, slowly but surely, finding her way back to the quiet life she had once craved, a life forever changed by the events that had thrust her into the national spotlight. She would always carry the weight of responsibility, but she would also carry the quiet pride of knowing that she had done what was necessary, that she had faced the darkness and emerged, stronger, into the light.

Dealing with Trauma

The immediate aftermath of the averted attack was a blur of adrenaline and exhaustion, a chaotic symphony of flashing lights, blaring sirens, and the relentless buzz of news helicopters overhead. But the moment the dust settled, the weight of the experience crashed down on Laila and her team with the force of a tidal wave. The heroism lauded by the media felt distant, a hollow echo in the face of the stark reality of what they had endured.

Sergeant Miller, Laila's closest confidante on the team, retreated into a shell of silence. His usually jovial demeanor was replaced by a haunted look, his eyes reflecting a deep weariness that went beyond physical fatigue. He would sit for hours, staring blankly at a wall, the events of that day replaying in his mind like a broken record. He'd flinch at loud noises, a jarring reminder of the chaotic crescendo of gunfire and explosions. Sleep became a luxury, replaced by nightmares that jolted him awake in cold sweats. The bravado that had served him so well on the battlefield was gone, replaced by a fragile vulnerability. He started drinking heavily, seeking solace in the bottom of a bottle, a self- destructive coping mechanism that worried Laila immensely.

Officer Davis, the youngest member of the team, displayed a different kind of trauma. While physically unharmed, he exhibited classic symptoms of PTSD: hypervigilance, anxiety attacks, and intrusive thoughts. He constantly scanned his surroundings, his hands trembling, his eyes darting nervously. Even in the relative safety of his own home, he felt threatened, vulnerable. Simple tasks, like going to the grocery store or answering the phone, became herculean efforts, draining him both physically and emotionally. He started having panic attacks, episodes of intense fear and shortness of breath that left him gasping for air, overwhelmed by a sense of impending doom.

For Laila, the trauma manifested in a different form. She experienced bouts of intense anger, a simmering rage that threatened to consume her. The frustration of almost losing her life, the anger at the terrorists for their callous disregard for human life, the exhaustion of the constant media scrutiny – it all built up inside her, a pressure cooker threatening to explode. She found herself snapping at her colleagues, her family, even strangers. The quiet intensity that had once been her strength was now a volatile force, unpredictable and frightening. She struggled to control it, the anger a constant shadow lurking at the edge of her consciousness.

The agency recognized the need for intervention. They arranged for the entire team to undergo intensive therapy sessions, facilitated by a team of experienced psychologists specializing in trauma. The sessions were grueling, forcing each member to confront the demons they carried within. They had to relive the horrors of that day, to dissect their responses, to unpack the emotional baggage that threatened to overwhelm them. It wasn't easy. There were tearful breakdowns, moments of intense anger and frustration, periods of agonizing silence. But through the process, they began to heal, to understand the nature of their trauma and to find ways to cope.

The therapy sessions were not a quick fix; it was a journey of self-discovery and healing, a process of slowly piecing themselves back together. Laila learned about the importance of self-care, the need to prioritize her well-being. She started practicing mindfulness techniques, finding solace in meditation and yoga, learning to ground herself in the present moment. She started taking long walks in the woods surrounding her farm, allowing nature to soothe her fractured spirit. She worked through her anger, finding healthy ways to process her emotions.

For Miller, the therapy sessions provided a space to confront his self-destructive habits. He learned about the importance of support, the need to talk to someone about his experiences, the necessity of facing his demons instead of running from them. He started attending Alcoholics Anonymous meetings, finding solace and support in a community of people who understood his struggles. He slowly started rebuilding his life, piece by piece, brick by brick.

Davis discovered the power of emotional expression, learning to articulate his feelings and experiences instead of bottling them up. He started journaling, using writing as a form of therapy, pouring out his anxieties and fears onto paper. He began practicing breathing exercises to manage his panic attacks, learning to regulate his emotions and regain control of his body. He found a support group for first responders, finding comfort in sharing his experiences with people who understood the unique challenges of their profession.

The road to recovery was long and arduous. There were setbacks, moments of despair, times when they felt like they were losing the battle. But they persevered, supporting each other, reminding each other of their strength, their resilience. They were a team, not only in the face of danger but also in the face of adversity. They were a band of brothers and sisters, bound by shared experiences, united in their struggle to heal.

The scars remained, invisible marks etched on their souls. But the scars were also a testament to their resilience, a

reminder of the battles they had fought and won. The trauma of that day would always be a part of them, but it would not define them. They had faced the darkness and emerged into the light, stronger and more connected than ever before.

Their experiences had forged an unbreakable bond, a deep understanding of the human spirit's capacity for both profound suffering and remarkable healing. The quiet moments of reflection, the shared laughter and tears, the mutual support—these were the true measures of their recovery, more valuable than any commendation or award. The city healed, and so did they, rebuilding their lives, their connections, and their sense of self. Their journey towards healing was far from over, but in their shared trauma, they found a strength that would endure. The memories of that day would forever be a part of them, but it would not define their future. They would carry on, facing the world with a newfound appreciation for life, love, and the enduring power of the human spirit. The city they had saved, in turn, had become their haven, a silent testament to their collective resilience and their shared triumph over adversity.

Laila's Personal Reflection

The city lights blurred through the rain-streaked window of my farmhouse. The silence was profound, a stark contrast to the cacophony of the past week. The media frenzy had subsided, the accolades fading into the background hum of daily life. But the echoes of gunfire, the screams, the raw terror – those remained, etched into the recesses of my memory. They were a constant, unwelcome companion, whispering in the quiet hours, intruding upon my dreams.

This wasn't the quiet peace I'd craved when I'd retreated to the farm after my divorce. This was a different kind of quiet, heavy with the weight of unspoken trauma. The quiet of a battlefield after the battle, where the smoke clears and you're left to confront the devastation. The farm, once a symbol of refuge, now felt like a battleground of a different kind, the enemy within.

My life had always been defined by action, by the adrenaline rush of high-stakes situations. The controlled chaos of combat, the calculated risks, the unwavering focus – that was my comfort zone. But this…this was different. This was the aftermath, the slow, agonizing process of healing, of coming to terms with the brutal reality of what I had faced.

The nightmares were relentless. I'd wake up screaming, drenched in sweat, my heart pounding like a drum. I would see the faces of the terrorists, their twisted grins, their eyes filled with a cold, hateful emptiness. I'd relive the heart- stopping moments, the near misses, the agonizing choices. The terror of being so close to death, the fear for my team, the crushing weight of responsibility…it all came crashing back with each nightmare.

During the day, the memories would intrude, unexpected flashbacks triggered by the most innocuous things – a car backfiring, a loud conversation, a news report about a similar incident. The world around me would shift, the present moment dissolving into a terrifying replay of the past. I'd find myself flinching, my hands trembling, my senses on high alert, expecting the next attack, even here, in the relative safety of my own home.

The anger was a constant companion too, a simmering volcano threatening to erupt at any moment. The anger at the terrorists, the rage at their senseless act of violence, the frustration at the near-misses, the bitterness of the constant media scrutiny...it was a toxic cocktail, eroding my peace and threatening to consume me. I had trouble sleeping, my mind racing, the images replaying in a continuous loop. I was jumpy, easily startled, even angered by the mundane inconveniences of daily life.

I tried to bury myself in work, throwing myself into investigations, hoping to drown out the noise in my head. But the silence between cases was the worst. In the quiet, the memories would return, sharper, more vivid than before. The faces of the fallen officers haunted me, their absence a constant reminder of the fragility of life.

The therapy sessions, though initially daunting, had started to help. Dr. Ramirez, a kind, insightful woman with a calm demeanor, had guided me through the labyrinth of my emotions, helping me to understand the nature of my trauma. She had helped me see that my anger wasn't a weakness, but a powerful force, a testament to my strength and resilience. She taught me how to channel that anger, to use it as fuel, to motivate me to keep fighting, to keep protecting others.

Learning to confront the trauma wasn't just about processing the past; it was about understanding my identity, my role in the world. Who was I, outside the confines of my military training, my law enforcement work? What did I want my life to look like, moving forward? These were questions I'd never really asked myself before, questions that had been pushed aside by duty, by ambition, by the relentless demands of my career.

Now, with the quiet of the aftermath, I was forced to confront these questions, to grapple with the complexities of my own identity. The woman who emerged from the smoke and flames of that harrowing day wasn't the same woman who had walked into the funeral procession. I was stronger, more resilient, but also more vulnerable, more aware of my own mortality.

The healing process wasn't linear. There were days when the pain was overwhelming, days when I felt like giving up. But I had my support system, my family, my friends, my colleagues. They were my anchors, the steady presence in the storm. They reminded me of my strength, my resilience, my value.

My connection with Sergeant Miller had deepened. We shared silent understanding, a bond forged in the crucible of shared trauma. He still struggled with the demons of PTSD, but he was fighting back, attending therapy, engaging in self- care. Seeing him fight, seeing his slow, gradual progress, gave me hope.

Officer Davis, too, was making strides. His

anxiety remained, but he was finding ways to manage it. He was writing poetry, expressing his pain and his fears through words. His work was powerful, raw, deeply emotional. It gave voice to the invisible wounds, the silent suffering.

Looking back, I realized that the battle against terrorism had been only one battle. The real war was the one I fought within myself, the ongoing struggle to heal, to rebuild, to rediscover my purpose. This was a different kind of combat, less about physical strength and more about inner resilience. This was a fight for my own soul, a fight I wouldn't give up on.

The farm, once a symbol of escape, now felt different. It was a place of healing, a sanctuary where I could reconnect with myself, with nature, with the quiet rhythms of life. The land seemed to absorb my pain, to offer a sense of grounding, a sense of calm. I started to spend more time outdoors, tending to the garden, walking through the woods. It helped to center me, to connect me with something larger than myself, something that transcended the chaos of my recent experiences.

The silence wasn't just the absence of sound; it was a space for reflection, a space for healing. The memories would always be there, but they wouldn't define me. They were a part of my story, a testament to my strength, my resilience, my unwavering commitment to justice. The scars I carried, both visible and invisible, were a reminder of the battles I had fought and won. And the quiet moments of reflection would become a source of strength, an unwavering support, reminding me that the city I'd saved was also the city that had quietly become my haven. The journey wasn't over, but in the quiet of the aftermath, I found a new kind of strength, a new understanding of myself, and a newfound appreciation for the simple things in life. The future remained uncertain, but I faced it not with fear, but with hope, renewed purpose, and the unwavering belief in the enduring power of the human spirit.

Legal Proceedings

The courtroom was a stark contrast to the chaos I'd recently endured. Instead of the adrenaline-fueled urgency of a terrorist threat, the air hung heavy with the methodical precision of the law. Rows of polished mahogany, the hushed whispers of spectators, the formal attire of the lawyers and the judge – it all felt strangely antiseptic, a sterile environment designed to dissect the raw brutality of the events I'd witnessed.

The defendants, led by the chillingly calm figure of Elias Thorne, sat at the defendant's table. Thorne, the mastermind behind the attack, his eyes held a disturbing lack of remorse, a coldness that sent a shiver down my spine even from across the vast expanse of the courtroom. His accomplices, a motley crew of disillusioned individuals, displayed a range of emotions; fear, defiance, and a chilling apathy. Their faces, etched with a mix of exhaustion and apprehension, mirrored the internal conflict raging within them.

My testimony was painstakingly detailed. I recounted the events of that fateful day, describing the meticulous planning, the chillingly efficient execution, and the near-misses that had almost cost the lives of countless officers. I meticulously detailed Thorne's leadership, his manipulative tactics, and the chilling indifference he displayed towards the potential loss of innocent lives. The prosecution, led by the sharp, relentless Sarah Chen, skillfully guided me through my narrative, ensuring every detail was presented with clarity and precision. Her questioning was pointed, her tone unwavering, reflecting her profound commitment to securing justice for the fallen officers and their families.

The defense team, a formidable group led by the silver- tongued, yet ruthless, Mark Holloway, attempted to cast doubt on my testimony, questioning my emotional state and suggesting the possibility of exaggeration or misinterpretation. Holloway's tactics were classic – attempting to undermine my credibility by highlighting the trauma I'd experienced, implying that my stress might have clouded my judgement and recollection. He presented character witnesses who painted Thorne as a misunderstood idealist, a man driven by righteous anger rather than cold-blooded malice.

However, Chen expertly countered Holloway's arguments, presenting irrefutable evidence from our investigation: intercepted communications, forensic evidence linking Thorne to the scene, the meticulously planned logistics of the attack. She showcased Thorne's history of extremist activities, highlighting his affiliations with known hate groups, his past violent offenses, and his meticulous preparation for the attack. Each piece of evidence, meticulously presented, chipped away at Holloway's carefully constructed defense.

The testimony of other officers, some shaken, some stoic, helped to corroborate my account. Sergeant Miller's account of the chaotic gun battle, his voice strained with the weight of his ordeal, delivered a visceral account of the terror and violence the terrorists had inflicted. Officer Davis, despite his visible nervousness, provided crucial details about Thorne's meticulous planning and the coordination with his accomplices. His shaky hands and trembling voice only underscored the gravity of the situation, lending a heartbreaking authenticity to his account.

The trial lasted for weeks, a grueling marathon of testimony, cross-examinations, and legal maneuvering. The courtroom became a battleground, not of bullets and bombs, but of words, meticulously chosen to dismantle the defense's narrative and present a compelling case for the prosecution. Each day felt like a fight, a relentless struggle to ensure that justice was served, to give voice to the victims, and to protect the city from future threats. The weight of responsibility was immense, the pressure immense. The lives of those fallen officers, and the hope for closure for their families, weighed heavily upon me.

The defense's attempts to portray the terrorists as victims of circumstance, manipulated by societal injustices, fell flat against the overwhelming evidence of their premeditation and callous disregard for human life. The chilling indifference with which they carried out their attacks, coupled with the extensive evidence of their planning, was simply too compelling to ignore.

One of the most heart-wrenching moments came during the testimony of the families of the fallen officers. Their grief, their raw anguish, the palpable loss they were still struggling to process – it was a powerful testament to the devastating impact of the terrorists' actions. Their words, laced with sorrow but also with a fierce determination to see justice done, resonated throughout the courtroom, bolstering the prosecution's case. Their quiet dignity and courageous testimony acted as a somber reminder of the price of terrorism.

The jury deliberated for several days, the tension in the courtroom palpable as we all awaited their verdict. The anticipation was almost unbearable, a tangible pressure that seemed to crackle in the air. Finally, the verdict came. Guilty on all counts. The room erupted. The families of the victims wept openly, embracing each other in a profound moment of collective relief. There was a tangible sense of justice being served, an acknowledgment that the efforts of law enforcement, and the sacrifices made, had not been in vain.

Elias Thorne, his face betraying no emotion, received the sentence without a word. Life imprisonment without the possibility of parole. His accomplices received similar sentences, varying according to their level of involvement and culpability.

The legal proceedings provided a sense of closure, a validation of the sacrifices made and the battles fought. It wasn't the adrenaline-fueled rush of combat, but it was a victory nonetheless. The justice system, imperfect as it might be, had done its job, holding those responsible for their crimes accountable. The battle for justice hadn't been fought in the streets or in the shadows; instead, it unfolded in the sterile atmosphere of a courtroom, one carefully constructed argument and piece of evidence at a time. Yet, the stakes remained just as high. The fight for justice was just as crucial, just as vital in its own way as the fight against the terrorists. The courtroom's methodical process had delivered the kind of justice that the chaos of that day had demanded.

It was a testament to the enduring strength of the rule of law, the unwavering commitment to accountability, and the profound hope for a safer future, one where the acts of violence such as those committed on that day wouldn't go unpunished. The victory felt different, quieter, but no less profound. It was a victory for the rule of law, a testament to the resilience of the system, and a powerful affirmation that even in the face of unimaginable horror, justice could prevail.

The legal proceedings were over, but my own personal journey was far from finished. The echoes of gunfire, the screams, the raw terror of that day would forever remain etched in my memory. But now, there was a sense of closure, a sense of completion, a belief that the wheels of justice had turned, and the perpetrators had been held accountable for their actions. The legal battle had been fought and won, but the personal battle for healing and understanding would continue for a long time to come. The city was safe, but the long journey of healing had only just begun. The scars I carried, the visible and the invisible, would forever remind me of the battles fought and won. The quiet moments of reflection, however, offered a renewed sense of purpose, a sense of calm in the aftermath of chaos. I knew that the world was a dangerous place, filled with threats that could strike at any time, and that my duty was far from over. But I could finally allow myself to feel a sense of quiet pride.

Justice had been served. And in that moment, the quiet victory felt profoundly important, profoundly meaningful.

Witness Testimony

The fluorescent lights of the courtroom hummed, a stark counterpoint to the echoing silence that preceded my testimony. I adjusted the microphone, the cold metal a jarring reminder of the chilling reality I was about to recount. My uniform, the crisp blue of a U.S. Marshal, felt strangely out of place in this formal setting, a stark contrast to the camouflage I'd worn during the harrowing events I was about to describe. The weight of the responsibility pressed down on me, a physical burden as heavy as the memories I carried.

Sarah Chen, the lead prosecutor, her face etched with a determined seriousness, leaned in. "Ms. Wright," she began, her voice calm but firm, "can you please recount the events of October 27th, beginning with your arrival at the memorial service?"

My heart hammered against my ribs, a frantic drumbeat against the quiet hum of the courtroom. I took a deep breath, trying to steady my nerves, to control the tremor in my hands. The memory of the day replayed in my mind, a vivid, agonizing slideshow of chaotic violence and near misses. I could still smell the acrid bite of cordite, the metallic tang of blood, and feel the phantom weight of my weapon in my hand.

"I arrived at the memorial service for Officer Miller," I began, my voice steady despite the internal turmoil, “around 10:00 AM. The atmosphere was somber, respectful, a stark contrast to what was about to unfold. I noticed a black SUV parked unusually close to the procession route, its tinted windows obscuring the occupants inside. Something about its position, its almost aggressive proximity, felt unsettlingly out of place. My instincts, honed by years of experience, screamed warning. It wasn't the usual respectful distance maintained by bystanders."

I described the seemingly innocuous details: the slight misalignment of the license plates, the subtle inconsistencies in the vehicle's markings that even a casual observer might miss. I recounted how my heightened awareness, a byproduct of my years in the Forsvarets Special Kommando and the U.S. Marshals Service, had flagged this seemingly insignificant detail as a major red flag. I had spent years learning to trust my gut, and in this instance, my gut was screaming.

"I discreetly alerted Sergeant Miller and Officer Davis of my concerns," I continued, "my suspicion growing with every passing moment. We exchanged a few words, enough to signal my apprehension but not enough to cause alarm amongst the mourners. Then, suddenly, chaos erupted.
Gunfire shattered the somber atmosphere, ripping through the air like a violent storm. The black SUV, the same one I'd been watching, sped into the procession, its occupants opening fire with ruthless precision. It was a calculated ambush, a meticulously planned attack."

My voice tightened with emotion as I described the ensuing carnage, the pandemonium that followed. The screams of the wounded officers, the desperate cries for help, the deafening roar of gunfire, all melded into a cacophony of terror. I recounted my own actions, the adrenaline-fueled response that kicked in as I engaged in a fierce firefight to protect the surviving officers. I detailed my tactical maneuvers, my efforts to neutralize the threat and create a safe zone for the injured. The memories were raw, painful, a stark reminder of the brutal reality of violence.

"I engaged Thorne and his accomplices in close-quarters combat," I explained, my voice strained but clear. "Thorne was particularly ruthless, cold, and efficient in his movements. He wielded his weapon with chilling precision. His eyes betrayed a disturbing absence of remorse, an almost clinical detachment from the carnage he was creating. His accomplices, though less skilled, were equally determined and dangerous."

My testimony included a detailed account of the firefight, the precise choreography of movements and responses, and the crucial decisions made under intense pressure. I meticulously described the terrorists' weapons, tactics, and their relentless assault. I demonstrated the lethality of their approach, highlighting the calculated nature of their attack. The courtroom, previously hushed, held its collective breath as I painted a vivid picture of the mayhem.

Mark Holloway, the defense attorney, rose to his feet, his silver hair glinting under the courtroom lights. His tone was suave, almost condescending, a calculated attempt to undermine my credibility. He questioned my emotional state, suggesting that stress could impair my recall. He pounced on every pause, every hesitation, attempting to sow seeds of doubt.

"Ms. Wright," he drawled, his voice dripping with sarcasm, "considering the intensity of the events you describe, isn't it possible that your recollection might be… somewhat… colored by the stress of the situation? Perhaps your adrenaline-fueled state might have distorted your perception of events?"

I met his gaze, unwavering. Years of training had prepared me for this kind of cross-examination, the relentless attacks designed to break down a witness's composure. I remained calm, my responses precise and unwavering.

"Sir," I replied, my voice steady and confident, "my training has equipped me to operate under intense pressure. While I acknowledge the stress I experienced that day, I can assure you that my recollection of the events is accurate and truthful. My observations were made under controlled observation, allowing for keen observation and accurate recollection." I meticulously detailed my tactical training, explaining the observational techniques that allowed me to process information effectively in high-stress environments.

The cross-examination continued for hours, a

relentless barrage of questions designed to discredit my account. Holloway attempted to portray me as emotionally unstable, suggesting that my trauma might have affected my perception of events. He questioned the details of my actions, attempting to find inconsistencies and contradictions. However, the meticulous nature of my testimony, its coherence and clarity, stood as a testament to my experience and to the accuracy of my recollection. Sarah Chen's deft handling of the re-direct examination further solidified my testimony. She presented additional evidence that corroborated my account, reinforcing the validity of my observations.

The courtroom remained silent as I completed my testimony, the weight of the events still heavy on my shoulders. My words hung in the air, a stark testament to the raw brutality of the day. My testimony had provided a comprehensive account of the terrorist attack, a detailed portrayal of the events that had unfolded. It was a recounting of violence and resilience, a battle fought not just in the streets but within the walls of the courtroom. The quiet hum of the fluorescent lights seemed to echo the quiet intensity of the moment, the weight of the truth I had delivered. The future, though uncertain, felt slightly less terrifying. Justice would have its say.

Facing the Press

The courtroom doors swung open, revealing a sea of flashing cameras and microphones. The air crackled with anticipation, a palpable energy that vibrated against my skin. My carefully tailored suit, a sharp contrast to the battlefield fatigues I often found myself in, felt strangely restrictive, almost suffocating. The weight of expectation pressed down on me, heavier than any flak jacket I'd ever worn. This was a different kind of combat, a battle fought not with bullets and bombs, but with words and images, a war for public perception.

Sarah Chen, ever the reassuring presence, placed a comforting hand on my arm. "Remember what we discussed," she murmured, her voice calm yet firm. "Stick to the facts, avoid emotional outbursts. Let your actions speak louder than any inflammatory rhetoric." Her words were a lifeline, a reminder to channel my military training and stay focused. Control. That was the key. The same control that had saved lives on the streets that day would be the instrument of my survival now.

Stepping onto the makeshift podium, the blinding flash of cameras momentarily stole my breath. I felt an instinctive flinch, a leftover reflex from years spent in combat zones where sudden bright lights signified danger. I fought the impulse, settling into a combat-ready stance, using the training that had become ingrained in my very being. The press conference felt like a battlefield, although the weapons were different.

The first question came, sharp and pointed, from a seasoned reporter with a skeptical glint in his eye. “Ms. Wright, some

are questioning your account of the events. The defense claims your actions were…excessive. Can you address these allegations?”

I met his gaze, unwavering. "My actions were in direct response to a deadly threat," I replied, my voice measured, controlled. "My training, both with the Forsvarets Special Kommando and the U.S. Marshals Service, prepared me to act decisively in situations demanding immediate and decisive intervention to prevent further loss of life. Every action I took was calculated, purposeful, and aimed at neutralizing the immediate threat. I saved lives that day, and if given the same circumstances, I would do it again.” I kept my tone even, avoiding any hint of emotional vulnerability. It was a calculated response, designed to diffuse the aggressive tone of the question without engaging in unnecessary confrontation.

The next volley of questions was a barrage—each more aggressive than the last. They probed my past, digging into my time in Norway, my marriage to Frank, even my reasons for leaving the army. They sought inconsistencies, contradictions, anything to cast doubt on my credibility.
They attempted to pry into the details of the firefight, seeking to create doubt where there was none. They questioned my emotional response. Some comments were aimed directly at undermining my authority. Others questioned my motives. Many were overtly sexist and dismissive of my stature, referencing my height and weight, as if to imply physical inadequacy.

Each question, each challenge, was a calculated strike. But I'd faced tougher opponents. My military training had prepared me for this kind of intense pressure. This press conference was merely a different type of battle. I deflected every personal attack with a controlled, professional response, focusing on the facts of the case and the tactical decisions I made. I acknowledged the personal struggles, but refrained from dwelling on the details. I didn't reveal anything personal, only professional.

A reporter from a national news network pressed me further, "Ms. Wright, your testimony yesterday was incredibly detailed. Some are suggesting your recollection is too precise, almost… staged. How can you account for such perfect recall?"

I calmly explained the rigorous training I'd undergone. "My training emphasized meticulous observation and accurate recall. We were taught to record every detail, to analyze every subtle nuance. It's not about perfect memory; it's about systematic observation, about training my mind to function as a high-performance tool, capable of processing a significant amount of information under extreme stress." I mentioned my training in tactical awareness, emphasizing the importance of remaining calm and focused under duress.

The questions continued, some probing my combat experience in Norway, others focusing on the specifics of the attack, and others attempting to paint a picture of me as someone who was unstable and emotionally charged. I answered each with the same calculated precision, sticking to the facts and avoiding any emotional displays. I highlighted the meticulous planning of the attack, the terrorists' ruthless efficiency, and the sheer brutality of the assault. I painted a grim picture of their callous disregard for human life.

Hours later, as the press conference finally ended, the exhaustion hit me like a physical blow. The adrenaline that had sustained me throughout began to wane, leaving a hollow ache in its place. I felt the weight of the day settle on

my shoulders, the burden of responsibility for the lives I had saved and the lives I could not save. I had won the battle, but the war for justice was far from over. The fight to bring these terrorists to justice was ongoing, and I was more determined than ever to see it through.

The flood of media coverage that followed was relentless, a tsunami of opinions, analyses, and speculations. Some lauded me as a hero, a symbol of courage and resilience.
Others questioned my motives, my methods, even my sanity. I navigated the storm of public opinion with a steely resolve, my responses carefully crafted, measured, and unwavering. I knew that the true test was not only surviving

the attack but also surviving the aftermath, the intense scrutiny, and the public debate that inevitably followed such a traumatic event. I would not let them break me. I would stand strong, confident in my actions and my unwavering commitment to justice. The scars, both physical and emotional, would serve as reminders of the day. They would also serve as fuel for the fight that lay ahead. Justice would prevail.

Public Recognition

The days following the press conference blurred into a whirlwind of activity. My phone rang incessantly, a cacophony of calls from news outlets, talk show hosts, and even some well-meaning individuals offering their support. Sarah, my ever-reliable rock, acted as my gatekeeper, meticulously filtering through the requests, shielding me from the relentless onslaught of media attention. She managed my schedule, coordinating interviews and appearances, while carefully controlling the narrative, ensuring that the focus remained on the facts of the case and not on sensationalizing my personal life. It was a delicate balancing act, a war fought on a different front, one that demanded an entirely different set of skills.

The initial wave of public support was overwhelming. I was hailed as a hero, a symbol of courage and resilience. My picture adorned the front pages of newspapers and magazines, my story dominating the evening news. Letters poured in, overflowing with gratitude and admiration.
Strangers stopped me on the street, their eyes reflecting a mixture of awe and gratitude. It was

humbling, yet strangely unsettling. The constant attention, the incessant scrutiny, began to feel suffocating.

The adulation, however, was not universal. A significant portion of the public, fueled by partisan media and online echo chambers, questioned my actions, casting doubt on my motives and attempting to paint me as a rogue operator.
Online forums and social media platforms became battlegrounds, where my every move was dissected, analyzed, and often, cruelly misrepresented. Anonymous accounts spread misinformation and conspiracy theories, undermining my credibility and attacking my character. The attacks were vicious, personal, and relentlessly targeted.
They went after my family, dredging up details from my past, attempting to exploit every vulnerability they could find.

One particularly vitriolic article in a national tabloid portrayed me as a power-hungry attention-seeker, suggesting my actions were motivated by a desire for fame and recognition rather than a commitment to justice. The article included fabricated details about my personal life, twisting minor incidents into major scandals designed to damage my reputation. It was a smear campaign, a calculated attempt to

discredit me in the eyes of the public. Reading it left a bitter taste in my mouth, a knot of anger tightening in my chest.
The article aimed to undermine my credibility and create doubt about my capabilities. They even attempted to question the accuracy of my account of events.

Sarah, ever vigilant, immediately sprang into action. She contacted the newspaper's editor, demanding a retraction and an apology. She also worked behind the scenes, contacting other news outlets to counter the tabloid's false narrative.
She knew that allowing the article to remain unchallenged would damage my reputation, potentially hindering my ability to effectively testify against the terrorists. The strategy involved focusing on facts and providing additional evidence to corroborate my accounts. We had to quickly and effectively fight back the false narrative.

The legal team, meanwhile, began to explore options for legal action against the tabloid. They meticulously reviewed the article, identifying specific inaccuracies and fabrications. We knew that taking legal action could be a lengthy and complex process, but it was a necessary step to protect my reputation and ensure accountability for the deliberate spread

of misinformation. We also decided to counter the negative press with positive press. We worked on reaching out to other news outlets and media personalities, highlighting the factual account of events and showcasing support from respected officials and other people.

The outpouring of support from law enforcement colleagues and officials from the U.S. Marshals Service was significant. Many expressed their confidence in my actions, publicly acknowledging my bravery and professionalism. Several high-ranking officials came to my defense, offering their unconditional support. Their testimonies offered strong evidence of my capabilities and professionalism. They also gave a strong statement against the tabloid article.

The legal battle dragged on, and the constant media scrutiny continued, creating an environment of constant pressure and stress. I tried to maintain a semblance of normalcy, focusing on my physical and mental health, and maintaining regular contact with my family and friends. I found solace in the support of my loved ones and sought professional counseling to help me cope with the emotional toll of the ordeal. This proved to be very beneficial.

One evening, while reflecting on the events of the past few weeks, I realized something profound: the public's perception of me was not the battle; it was the battlefield. The war was not against terrorists, but against the manipulation of information, against the relentless spread of misinformation, and the blatant disregard for truth. This realization gave me a new perspective, a renewed sense of purpose. The fight for justice would extend beyond the courtroom, extending to the fight for truth in the public sphere. This fight would be on multiple fronts.

The subsequent weeks brought a series of appearances on national television, radio interviews, and speaking engagements at various law enforcement conferences. Each engagement was an opportunity to reinforce my account of the events, to correct the misinformation, and to share my perspective with a wider audience. It wasn't just about clearing my name; it was about educating the public, countering the narrative of the terrorists, and ensuring that their actions would not be excused or minimized. I spoke passionately, sharing details of the attack and the terrorists' meticulous planning and cold-blooded disregard for human life. I aimed to humanize the victims, to remind the audience that these were not simply statistics but individuals who had loved ones, dreams, and futures that had been tragically cut short.

Throughout this period, I had to develop a new set of skills —skills in public speaking, media relations, and crisis communication. I learned to frame my answers carefully, to deflect inflammatory questions, and to control the narrative without resorting to emotional outbursts or inflammatory rhetoric. I recognized the importance of projecting calmness, confidence, and control, mirroring the demeanor I employed during the press conference, but this time, I realized I was not just battling the media; I was battling to ensure that this never happened again.

The legal battle concluded with a resounding victory. The tabloid was forced to retract the article, publish a full apology, and pay substantial damages for the harm caused. More importantly, this victory was a testament to the importance of fighting for truth and accountability. The legal proceedings helped ensure the public could differentiate between fact and fabricated information. It provided strong evidence of the importance of factual reporting and the potential dangers of irresponsible journalism. This helped set a clear precedent for future cases. The fight, however, did not end there. The trial against the terrorists would be the culmination of the fight. It was the culmination of many months of effort and planning. I was ready to ensure justice was served.

Dealing with Scrutiny

The exhaustion settled in like a physical weight, a constant companion in the weeks that followed. Sleep became a luxury I could rarely afford, my mind a relentless reel of the press conference, the interviews, the endless stream of faces blurred into a sea of expectation and judgment. The initial wave of public support, the outpouring of gratitude, had begun to recede, replaced by a tidal wave of scrutiny, a relentless barrage of questions, accusations, and outright attacks.

My apartment, usually a sanctuary, felt like a pressure cooker. The constant ringing of the phone, the insistent buzz of notifications on my tablet, were relentless intrusions.
Even the quiet moments were filled with an unsettling hum of anxiety, a low-level thrum of anticipation, waiting for the next blow to land. Sarah remained my unwavering shield, filtering calls, managing my schedule, and meticulously crafting my public responses, a tireless warrior battling my battles on a different front.

One evening, amidst the chaos, I found myself

staring at a photograph on my desk—a picture of me and Frank, taken during a trip to Norway, our faces lit by the ethereal glow of the Northern Lights. The memory of his smile, the warmth of his presence, was a sharp contrast to the icy coldness of the public scrutiny I was currently enduring. The divorce had been brutal, a battlefield of its own, but this felt different.

This wasn't a personal conflict; it was a public spectacle.

The attacks weren't confined to the mainstream media. The internet had become a toxic swamp, a breeding ground for conspiracy theories and personal attacks. Anonymous accounts, shielded by the veil of anonymity, unleashed a torrent of vitriol, twisting my words, misrepresenting my actions, and digging up details from my past, attempting to create a narrative that would discredit me. They went after my family, targeting my parents, my sister—anyone who might be vulnerable to their attacks.

One particular comment, buried deep within a thread on a far-right forum, chilled me to the bone. It mentioned my sister's address, a detail I had never shared publicly. The anonymity afforded by the internet offered a license for malice, a place where hatred could fester and spread unchecked. It was a chilling reminder of the reach of this digital darkness. Sarah immediately alerted the authorities, and extra measures were taken to ensure the safety of my family.

The legal team was working tirelessly, exploring options for legal action against the worst offenders. They faced a daunting task, trying to navigate the murky waters of online anonymity and fighting back against the sheer volume of misinformation. It was a war fought on multiple fronts, a relentless campaign to protect my reputation and ensure the accuracy of the information being shared.

Amidst the storm, the support of my colleagues was a lifeline. The Marshals Service rallied behind me, issuing statements of support, publicly backing my actions and refuting the false narratives being spread. The camaraderie of my fellow officers, their unwavering belief in my integrity, provided a sense of solidarity, a reassuring reminder that I was not alone in this fight.

But even their support couldn't completely buffer the emotional toll. The constant pressure, the relentless scrutiny, began to chip away at my resilience. The insomnia worsened, replaced by nightmares where the faces of the terrorists morphed into the faces of my critics. I found myself withdrawing, isolating myself even from those closest to me, fearing that my struggles would somehow reflect negatively on them.

Dr. Ramirez, my therapist, helped me to navigate these turbulent waters. Her calm demeanor and insightful observations helped me to reframe the situation, to view the public scrutiny not as a personal attack, but as a challenge, a battle to be fought with the same tactical precision I had employed on the battlefield. She encouraged me to focus on self-care, to prioritize my physical and mental health, reminding me that resilience wasn't about being impervious to suffering but about the ability to recover and adapt.

The process of recovery was slow, gradual. I started small, re-introducing routines into my life—regular exercise, healthy eating, even something as simple as a quiet evening spent reading. Each small victory, each step forward, felt like a triumph against the overwhelming tide of negativity. I learned to compartmentalize, to separate the public persona from my private self, to create a mental space where the noise of the outside world could be muted, allowing me to focus on healing and self-care.

The legal battles continued, culminating in a series of court victories that forced retractions and apologies from several news outlets. It was a lengthy and exhausting process, but it was crucial in establishing the truth and ensuring accountability for those who had deliberately spread misinformation. The legal successes, however, did little to diminish the lingering anxiety and exhaustion.

I realized that the fight wasn't just about clearing my name; it was about combating the culture of misinformation and disinformation that had created such a toxic environment. It was a broader battle against the forces that seek to manipulate public opinion, to sow discord, and to undermine truth.

This realization gave me a new perspective, a renewed sense of purpose. The fight for justice extended beyond the courtroom, beyond the headlines. It was a battle fought in the public square, a war of narratives and counter-narratives, a struggle for the truth. I found myself driven by a desire to use my experience and platform to educate the public, to help others understand the challenges of fighting disinformation, and to empower them to become more discerning consumers of information in a world increasingly saturated with falsehoods. The fight for justice, I realized, was a lifelong commitment, a continuous struggle against the forces that sought to obscure the truth. And I was ready for the fight.

Lingering Questions

The courtroom victories, while satisfying, felt strangely hollow. The apologies issued by the news outlets, the retractions of their false narratives, were a balm to my wounded reputation, but they couldn't erase the scars left by the ordeal. The exhaustion lingered, a persistent shadow clinging to the edges of my days. Sleep remained elusive, haunted by fragments of nightmares and the echo of hateful voices. The digital venom, once unleashed, seemed impossible to fully contain. Even with legal victories secured, the whispers continued, the shadows lurked in the digital corners of the internet, a constant reminder of the fragility of truth in the age of misinformation.

One of the most unsettling aspects of the entire affair was the anonymity of my attackers. The internet, a tool of immense power and connection, had also become a weapon, a shield for those who wished to inflict harm from the safety of their keyboards. The legal team had managed to identify and prosecute some of the most egregious offenders, those who had actively targeted my family, but the vast majority remained hidden behind pseudonyms and proxies, their identities obscured by a carefully constructed labyrinth of digital anonymity. This sense of impunity, the feeling that justice was incomplete, gnawed at me.

Sarah, my rock throughout this ordeal, remained steadfast in her support, but even she seemed weary. The constant vigilance, the meticulous monitoring of online activity, the tireless effort to protect my family and me from the digital deluge, had taken its toll. Her unwavering dedication had been instrumental in navigating the storm, but the relentless pressure had begun to wear her down. I saw the exhaustion in her eyes, the weight of responsibility etched onto her face. She deserved a rest, a chance to step away from the relentless battle.

The investigation into the terrorist plot itself also left many questions unanswered. While we had successfully prevented the planned attack at the police memorial, the full extent of the conspiracy remained unclear. Were there other cells operating? Were there more planned attacks? The captured terrorists, though cooperative in revealing their immediate plans, remained tight-lipped about the broader network, their allegiances, and their ultimate goals. Their silence was a chilling testament to the sophistication and secrecy of the organization.

The lead investigator, a seasoned FBI agent named David Miller, a man whose stoicism masked a sharp intellect, shared my concerns. We spent countless hours poring over intelligence reports, analyzing intercepted communications, and chasing down leads, but each breakthrough seemed to lead to a new set of unanswered questions. The elusive nature of the terrorist network, their ability to operate undetected for so long, hinted at a larger, more complex conspiracy than we had initially anticipated. It was a frustrating, maddening game of cat and mouse, where every step forward seemed to be met with two steps back.

The lack of definitive answers fueled the conspiracy theories swirling online. My own involvement in thwarting the attack became a source of speculation, a canvas upon which wild, unsubstantiated narratives were painted. Some claimed I was a double agent, working with the terrorists. Others suggested I was involved in a cover-up, protecting powerful individuals within the government. The absurd nature of these claims only served to highlight the pervasive power of misinformation, its ability to twist facts, to create alternative realities that were completely detached from the truth. The digital echo chamber amplified these falsehoods, giving them a veneer of legitimacy that they simply did not deserve.

The psychological toll of the unresolved issues continued to weigh heavily upon me. The therapy sessions with Dr.
Ramirez provided a much-needed outlet, a safe space to process my emotions and confront the lingering anxieties. She helped me to understand that the unresolved questions were not a personal failure, but a reflection of the complex and often frustrating nature of fighting terrorism. The fight against terrorism, she explained, was rarely a neat and tidy affair with clear beginnings and endings. Often, the pursuit of justice was a protracted battle, filled with setbacks, uncertainties, and unanswered questions.

But her words, though insightful, didn't erase the gnawing uncertainty. The images of the terrorist attack, the near-miss, the faces of the officers who could have been victims, haunted my sleep. The weight of responsibility, the knowledge that countless lives had hung in the balance, settled heavily upon my shoulders. It was a burden I carried, a reminder that even in victory, there were losses, both seen and unseen.

The support of my colleagues within the Marshals Service was my constant lifeline. They rallied around me, providing a much-needed sense of camaraderie, reminding me that I was not alone in this struggle. Their unwavering support helped me to navigate the emotional turmoil, to find strength in the collective spirit of the service. They understood the challenges I faced, the psychological toll of fighting terrorism, and the complexities of a world where truth seemed increasingly elusive.

Yet, the lingering questions remained. The silence of the captured terrorists, the anonymity of many of my online attackers, the unresolved aspects of the terrorist plot itself—these unanswered questions created a sense of unease, a persistent hum of unresolved tension. It was this unresolved tension that drove me forward, that fueled my determination to find answers, to ensure that justice, however incomplete, would be served. The fight was far from over. The case, though ostensibly closed, felt like a door that had been slammed shut, leaving behind the quiet rustle of unresolved issues, the whisper of secrets yet to be revealed. The story, it seemed, was far from finished. It was a story that continued to unfold, a tale with many chapters yet to be written, a battle still in progress, the lingering questions a stark reminder of the ongoing war against the darkness. And I, Laila Aurora Wright, was ready to face whatever challenges lay ahead, to seek the truth, wherever it may lead, armed with nothing but my skills, my determination, and the unwavering support of my colleagues. The fight continues. The hunt is far from over.

Unforeseen Consequences

The celebratory mood following the thwarted terrorist attack at the police memorial quickly dissipated, replaced by a chilling realization: the victory was far from complete. The arrests, while significant, felt like capturing only a few splinters from a vast, insidious network. The captured terrorists, initially forthcoming about their immediate plans, clammed up like oysters, their silence a fortress against further interrogation. Agent Miller, my steadfast ally in the FBI, and I were left staring into a void, a frustrating abyss of unanswered questions. The lack of information felt like a gaping wound, a constant reminder of the shadowy forces still at large.

One unexpected consequence was the media's insatiable appetite for a narrative, even if it was a distorted one. My role in preventing the massacre had initially been hailed as heroic, but the absence of complete information fueled speculation. News channels, in their desperate pursuit of ratings, began weaving narratives that bordered on fantastical, drawing connections to long-discredited conspiracy theories and suggesting that the entire event was an elaborate government operation, a cover-up to conceal something far more sinister. My personal life, already vulnerable due to my high-profile divorce from Frank, was subjected to an even more intense level of scrutiny. False stories began to circulate – rumors of illicit affairs, hidden agendas, and ties to shadowy organizations. The viciousness of these attacks, hidden behind the cloak of anonymity the internet provided, shocked even me. I had faced enemy fire and hand-to-hand combat, but the weaponized falsehoods felt like a different kind of war, a relentless assault on my character and reputation.

The digital attacks were relentless. Social media was ablaze with fabricated accusations, each post a tiny flame adding to a raging inferno of misinformation. My phone buzzed incessantly with hateful messages, anonymous threats, and doctored images that attempted to portray me in the worst possible light. Sarah, my unwavering support system, fought tirelessly to counter the negative narratives, employing every legal avenue available to address the malicious content. Her efforts, however, were like trying to stem the flow of a river with a teacup. The sheer volume of disinformation was overwhelming, constantly outpacing our ability to counter it. She was exhausted, depleted, her face etched with the fatigue of a battle fought without end. I watched, helpless, as the weight of the situation pressed down on her, a heavy cloak of responsibility.

The lack of closure regarding the terrorist plot, coupled with the unrelenting media frenzy and the digital attacks, created a ripple effect impacting my personal life. My relationship with my family was strained. My parents, initially proud of my achievements, were now consumed with worry, constantly bombarded by the negative news and fearful for my safety. My close friends, worried for my well-being, began to distance themselves, overwhelmed by the toxic atmosphere and the sheer intensity of the public scrutiny.
The isolation felt like a physical weight, adding to the exhaustion and stress.

The psychological impact was profound. The nightmares intensified, vivid scenes of the almost-massacre replaying in my mind. I found myself flinching at sudden noises, constantly scanning my surroundings for threats. Dr. Ramirez, my therapist, diagnosed me with acute PTSD, a testament to the trauma I had endured. The therapy sessions became a lifeline, but the sessions were grueling.
Working

through the layers of emotional pain, confronting the suppressed memories of near-death experiences, the feeling of helplessness as I nearly failed to stop the massacre, was a difficult process. The unresolved issues of the case, however, continued to weigh on me, preventing the kind of healing I so desperately craved. The unanswered questions acted as a constant reminder of my incompleted mission, of the potential for a future attack that I might fail to prevent.

The strain on my colleagues was also palpable. The Marshals Service, usually a bastion of stability and support, had become a place of tension. The aftermath of the event had shaken the confidence of some officers. The near-miss at the police memorial served as a stark reminder of the ever- present threat to their lives and the lives of their families.
Morale was low, and the usual camaraderie was replaced with a sense of unease and apprehension. We worked longer hours, with greater intensity, each one of us feeling the burden of responsibility weigh heavily upon our shoulders. The ever-present threat of another attack hung over us like a dark cloud, casting a shadow over every aspect of our lives.

The investigation continued, but progress remained agonizingly slow. Agent Miller and I chased every lead, however improbable. We spent countless nights poring over intelligence reports, analyzing intercepted communications, and interviewing potential witnesses. Each breakthrough, however small, was met with a renewed sense of hope, only to be dashed against the wall of the terrorist organization's secrecy. The network was like a hydra, with many heads, each one seemingly independent, yet connected by unseen threads. Each time we thought we were closing in, we would discover a new, previously unknown branch of the operation, expanding the scale and complexity of the threat.

The unforeseen consequences also extended to the legal sphere. Lawsuits against the media organizations that had published the false narratives began to drag on, a slow and painstaking process. Despite the legal victories, the damage had already been done. The damage to my reputation, the emotional toll on my family, and the strain on my professional relationships would take years to heal.

The events surrounding the police memorial attack had revealed a terrifying reality: that the fight against terrorism is not a single battle, but a protracted war fought on multiple fronts. The physical battle is only one part. The battle against misinformation, the psychological toll on individuals and communities, and the constant shadow of future threats – these are equally significant aspects of the war. The victory at the memorial, while undeniably important, had come at a heavy price, highlighting the unforeseen consequences that ripple outwards from even the most successful interventions. The fight continues, not just against the terrorists themselves, but against the insidious spread of misinformation, the deep psychological scars of trauma, and the enduring threat of future attacks. The hunt was far from over. The war was far from won.

New Threats Emerge

The chilling silence from the captured terrorists wasn't the only unsettling development. A new wave of threats, far more insidious than the initial attack, began to emerge.
Agent Miller and I found ourselves chasing shadows, each lead a tantalizing glimpse into a vast, interconnected network of domestic extremism that seemed to grow more complex with every passing day.

Our initial investigation had focused on a small, seemingly isolated cell. Now, intelligence reports painted a picture far more disturbing: a sprawling, decentralized network, with cells operating independently across multiple states, each with its own unique agenda, yet bound together by a shared ideology of anti-government sentiment and white supremacist beliefs. The internet, a tool initially used for communication and recruitment, had become the organization's digital fortress, allowing them to operate in the shadows, shielded from traditional law enforcement methods. Encrypted messaging apps, dark web forums, and anonymous online communities allowed them to communicate securely, plan operations, and recruit new members without leaving a digital trail.

One particularly troubling development was the discovery of several underground arms caches scattered across the country. These weren't just isolated stashes of weapons; they were well-stocked arsenals, containing enough firepower to launch a coordinated attack on a scale far greater than the one we had narrowly averted. The sheer scale of the operation shocked even seasoned veterans like myself. The sophistication of their planning, their ability to move undetected, and their access to advanced weaponry indicated a level of organization that far surpassed anything we had anticipated. It suggested a shadowy funding source, an unseen hand pulling the strings, a puppet master operating from the shadows.

The intelligence also revealed a disturbing trend: the increasing radicalization of individuals through online propaganda. Hate speech, conspiracy theories, and extremist rhetoric circulated freely online, creating a fertile breeding ground for violence and intolerance. The internet had become a powerful tool for recruiting vulnerable individuals, often those feeling marginalized or disenfranchised, and manipulating them into committing acts of violence. This digital radicalization was a far more pervasive and difficult threat to counter than any traditional terrorist organization.

To complicate matters further, the network wasn't solely focused on large-scale attacks. The intelligence pointed to a pattern of smaller-scale acts of violence – targeted killings of law enforcement officials, vandalism of government buildings, and cyberattacks against critical infrastructure.
These seemingly isolated incidents, initially dismissed as unrelated, were revealed to be part of a broader strategy, a systematic campaign designed to destabilize society and sow chaos. The strategy was reminiscent of a slow-burning fuse, designed to gradually erode public trust and incite widespread fear and uncertainty.

The psychological warfare aspect of their operation was equally concerning. The fabricated narratives and online smear campaigns against me were only the tip of the iceberg. We uncovered evidence suggesting that the terrorists had been deliberately spreading misinformation and disinformation through various online channels to create confusion, undermine public trust in law enforcement, and discredit the government. Their strategy was designed to sow discord and paranoia, exploiting existing societal divisions to further their own agenda.

Agent Miller and I were working tirelessly, piecing together the fragmented information, attempting to connect the dots and build a comprehensive understanding of the enemy. We were aided by a small team of analysts, linguists, and cyber specialists from the FBI, all working around the clock, but the challenge was immense. The sheer volume of data, the complexity of the network, and the sophistication of their methods made it feel like trying to solve a massive, ever- shifting jigsaw puzzle with missing pieces.

The pressure was immense. We were racing against time, trying to prevent another catastrophic attack before it could happen. Sleep became a luxury, meals were snatched on the run, and the weight of responsibility felt like a physical burden, pressing down on our shoulders. The psychological toll was significant; the constant fear of another attack, the knowledge of the impending danger, and the immense pressure to succeed created a constant state of anxiety and tension.

But amidst the chaos and uncertainty, there were glimmers of hope. A breakthrough in the investigation came in the form of a seemingly insignificant detail – a specific type of encrypted messaging app used exclusively by several members of the terrorist network. Through meticulous analysis of intercepted communications and a covert operation involving an undercover agent who had successfully infiltrated one of the smaller cells, we were able to identify the app's vulnerabilities and gain access to their encrypted communications. The information we uncovered was explosive, revealing the location of several previously unknown arms caches, the identities of key leaders within the network, and details of their future plans.

The information also revealed a troubling connection to a far more significant player – a shadowy international organization known only as "The Serpent's Hand," believed to be involved in arms trafficking and funding extremist groups across the globe. This connection raised the stakes considerably, transforming the investigation from a domestic terrorism case into a major international incident. The implications were staggering. The network we had been investigating was not merely a group of domestic extremists; it was a pawn in a much larger, more sinister game. Our local problem had become a global issue.

The discovery of this link forced a recalibration of our strategy. The FBI's involvement expanded significantly, with multiple agencies – including the CIA and the Department of Homeland Security – joining the investigation. International cooperation became crucial, requiring the delicate negotiation of agreements with foreign governments to facilitate intelligence sharing and joint operations. The scale and complexity of the investigation had dramatically increased, demanding more resources and expertise. The pressure intensified, but so did our determination.

The unfolding situation highlighted a stark and sobering reality: the war against terrorism was a multifaceted challenge, extending far beyond the battlefield. It required a coordinated effort involving law enforcement, intelligence agencies, and international cooperation, combined with a comprehensive strategy to combat the spread of extremism online. The enemy was adaptable and persistent, always evolving and adapting to our methods. The fight would be long, and the challenges would be immense. But the stakes were too high to fail. The hunt for the Serpent's Hand and the dismantling of the terrorist network had become the most

critical mission of my career. And I was determined to succeed.

Personal Conflicts

The adrenaline had finally faded, leaving behind a gnawing emptiness that no amount of coffee could fill. The successful thwarting of the terrorist attack felt less like a victory and more like a reprieve, a temporary stay of execution in a war with no clear end. The weight of what I'd witnessed, the near misses, the sheer brutality of it all, settled heavily on my chest, a suffocating blanket of exhaustion and dread. Sleep offered little respite; nightmares plagued me, vivid replays of the carnage, the screams, the faces of the fallen. I would wake in a cold sweat, heart pounding, the taste of fear bitter on my tongue.

The farm, once a sanctuary, now felt like a cage. The quiet solitude, once comforting, was now a deafening reminder of the chaos I'd left behind. The rolling hills, the whispering cornfields, they all seemed to mock my attempts at peace, whispering of the violence I had barely escaped. Even the familiar scent of hay and earth couldn't mask the metallic tang of blood that seemed permanently etched in my memory.

My divorce from Frank still hung heavy in the air, an unresolved wound that festered in the silence of the farmhouse. The pain wasn't just the loss of a marriage; it was the loss of a shared history, a partnership forged in the crucible of a foreign battlefield. Norway held both the most beautiful and the most horrific memories of my life, a country inextricably linked to Frank and to the very skills that had saved lives, skills that now haunted me. Our shared experiences, once a bond of unbreakable strength, now felt like a cruel irony, a constant reminder of what I had lost.

The investigation, far from offering closure, had opened new wounds. The constant threat, the ever-present danger, the sheer scale of the conspiracy, it chipped away at my resolve, slowly eroding my confidence. Doubt gnawed at the edges of my certainty; was I truly capable of handling this? Had I missed something? Could I have prevented the attack entirely? The questions, unanswered and unanswerable, haunted me day and night. The responsibility for the lives I'd saved, the lives I'd failed to save, weighed me down like an anchor.

Agent Miller, a veteran himself, seemed to understand the silent battle raging within me. He'd seen his share of darkness, experienced the same chilling aftermath of violence and loss. He wasn't one for empty platitudes or forced camaraderie; instead, he offered a quiet, unwavering support, a knowing glance across the room, a shared cup of coffee in the dead of night. He knew the war didn't end with the capture of the terrorists; it continued within the walls of our own minds.

The physical toll was equally significant. My body ached, a constant reminder of the adrenaline-fueled battles, the sleep deprivation, and the relentless pressure. The strain of the investigation had exacerbated old injuries; the lingering pain in my shoulder, a souvenir from a training exercise gone wrong in Norway, throbbed incessantly. The muscle fatigue was so debilitating I sometimes felt I was moving through life under water, weighed down by an invisible force.

Even simple tasks felt monumental, exhausting. The farm chores, once a welcome distraction, now seemed insurmountable obstacles. The simplest act of chopping vegetables for dinner turned into a herculean effort, my hands shaking, my movements slow and deliberate, my mind still wrestling with the aftermath of the attack.

My therapist, Dr. Alvarez, a woman who had treated numerous soldiers returning from combat, understood the nuances of my struggle. She didn't try to minimize my pain or offer quick fixes; instead, she offered a safe space to unpack the trauma, to confront the nightmares and the ghosts of my past. She helped me understand that the feelings of anxiety, the flashbacks, the nightmares, were not signs of weakness but rather the body's natural response to extreme stress. She encouraged me to engage in activities that brought me peace, even if only for short periods, reminding me that self-care wasn't selfish but crucial for survival.

The quiet moments on the farm, watching the sunset paint the sky in hues of orange and purple, gradually became less painful, less like a cruel reminder of what I'd lost, and more like a solace, a brief respite from the storm within. The familiar rhythm of farm life, the tending to the animals, the work of the land, slowly began to ground me, anchoring me to the present, reminding me of the simple joys that life still offered.

Yet, despite the progress, the scars remained, both visible and invisible. The visible ones were the physical reminders: the scars on my arms and legs from past engagements; the lingering aches and pains that plagued my body. The invisible scars were far more insidious, the psychological wounds that ran deeper than skin. The constant vigilance, the hyper-awareness of my surroundings, the jumpiness at sudden noises, the recurring nightmares, they were a constant reminder of the life I'd left behind, the life that had irrevocably changed me.

The guilt lingered; a persistent shadow that followed me everywhere. The guilt of surviving, of witnessing the death of others, of not being able to save everyone. The guilt of leaving Frank behind, not only in a broken marriage but in a life that both of us had thought would be together. The guilt gnawed at my conscience, a relentless voice whispering doubts and uncertainties.

But amidst the darkness, there were flickers of hope, small rays of light piercing through the clouds of trauma. The support of Agent Miller, the understanding of Dr. Alvarez, the quiet solace of the farm, they all helped me navigate the treacherous terrain of my emotional landscape. The progress was slow, painstakingly slow, but it was progress nonetheless. The journey was far from over, the scars remained, but I was beginning to find a path forward, a way to live with the ghosts of

my past while embracing the fragile hope of a future. The fight was far from over, but the war within me, that was a battle I was determined to win.
The battle for peace started within, and slowly, I began to reclaim that peace, one sunrise at a time, one breath at a time.

The investigation continued, its tentacles stretching across states and continents. But for now, my focus was on myself, on healing, on finding a new equilibrium in a world that had irrevocably changed. The farm, once a symbol of escape, had become a crucible of healing, a place where I could begin the long and arduous process of piecing together the shattered fragments of my life, of learning to live with the invisible scars, and of finding a path forward, one small step at a time. The fight against the terrorists was ongoing, but my personal war, my battle for healing, that was a fight I had to win, for myself.

Rebuilding Her Life

The scent of woodsmoke and damp earth, once a comfort, now felt strangely alien. My hands, calloused from years of handling weapons and wrestling suspects, now trembled as I attempted to plant a simple row of tulips. The bulbs, small and fragile, felt like a metaphor for my own shattered state. I was trying to cultivate something beautiful from the wreckage of my life, but the ground felt hard, unyielding, resistant to the tender shoots of hope I was desperately trying to coax forth.

Dr. Alvarez had suggested gardening as a form of therapy, a way to connect with something larger than my own internal turmoil. She spoke of the grounding effect of the earth, the slow, deliberate rhythm of tending to plants as a counterpoint to the frenetic pace of my past life. But the rhythmic motion of the trowel felt more like a ritualistic act of penance, each bulb a tiny tomb for a buried memory.

Agent Miller's visits became less frequent, but no less impactful. He didn't pry, didn't offer unsolicited advice. His presence was a silent reassurance, a quiet affirmation that I wasn't alone in this struggle. He understood the invisible wounds, the lingering echoes of violence that reverberated within me. He'd seen the same haunted look in the eyes of other veterans, the same flickering shadow of trauma that clung to them like a second skin. We shared coffee, mostly in silence, the unspoken understanding passing between us like a current of shared experience.

The silence on the farm, once a source of anxiety, began to settle into something different, something akin to peace. It wasn't the absence of noise but the absence of the internal

cacophony, the relentless barrage of memories and anxieties that had previously dominated my consciousness. The quiet hum of the refrigerator, the creak of the old farmhouse settling, the rustling of leaves in the wind—these became the sounds of healing, the soundtrack to my slow, painstaking recovery.

I found solace in the simple routines of farm life. The milking of the cows, the feeding of the chickens, the tending to the garden—these mundane tasks became anchors, grounding me in the present moment, pulling me back from the swirling vortex of my memories. The physical exertion, the demanding nature of the work, served as a healthy distraction, a way to channel the pent-up energy and frustration that still simmered beneath the surface.

The physical therapy was slow and arduous. The shoulder injury, exacerbated by the recent events, was proving stubborn. The pain was a constant companion, a nagging reminder of the physical toll my life had taken. But the sessions, while painful, were also a source of strength, a testament to my resilience. Each small victory, each incrementally improved range of motion, was a triumph over the physical limitations imposed by my injuries.

Sleep remained elusive, the nightmares continuing to plague my nights. But I began to find ways to manage them, to navigate the treacherous terrain of my dreams. Dr. Alvarez had introduced me to techniques of mindfulness and meditation, teaching me to observe my thoughts and feelings without judgment, to let them pass through me like clouds in the sky. It was a slow process, but gradually, I began to gain a sense of control over the chaos within my mind.

The process of healing wasn't linear. There were days when the pain overwhelmed me, days when the memories felt too raw, too vivid, too close. On those days, I would retreat to the solitude of the barn, finding comfort in the familiar smell of hay and the comforting presence of the animals. Their quiet acceptance, their uncritical gaze, offered a form of solace I couldn't find anywhere else.

I started to journal, pouring my thoughts and feelings onto paper, unburdening myself of the weight of unspoken emotions. The act of writing, of transforming the chaos within into coherent words, was surprisingly cathartic. It was a way to make sense of my experiences, to find meaning amidst the pain and suffering.

The legal proceedings against the terrorists dragged on, a slow, grinding process that tested my patience and my resolve. But I found a strange sense of satisfaction in witnessing the wheels of justice slowly turning, in seeing those responsible for the violence held accountable for their actions. It wasn't closure, not in the true sense of the word, but it was a step forward, a recognition that the events weren't simply forgotten or ignored. The fight for justice was far from over, but the legal process gave a sense of order and accountability to the chaos.

One evening, as the sun dipped below the horizon, painting the sky in shades of fiery orange and deep purple, I sat on the porch, a cup of warm tea in my hands. The quiet stillness of the evening, the gentle breeze rustling through the trees, the distant sound of crickets chirping—these simple things brought a sense of peace that had eluded me for so long.

The scars remained, both visible and invisible. The physical scars served as a reminder of my past experiences, a testament to the battles I had fought and survived. The invisible scars were more elusive, more insidious, the psychological wounds that ran deeper than skin. But as the sun set on another day, I realized that the scars didn't define me. They were a part of my story, but not the entirety of it. They were a testament to my resilience, a symbol of the battles I had won and the battles I would continue to fight.

Rebuilding my life wasn't about erasing the past; it was about integrating it, learning to live with the memories, the pain, the trauma. It was about finding a new equilibrium, a new sense of purpose, a new way of being in the world. The farm, once a refuge from the chaos of my past life, had become a crucible of healing, a place where I could confront my demons and emerge stronger, more resilient, more whole. The road ahead was long and uncertain, but I was finally ready to walk it, one step at a time, one sunrise at a time. The peace wasn't a destination, but a process, a journey of self-discovery and healing. And that journey, I knew, was just beginning. The quiet strength I found in myself, unexpected yet profoundly satisfying, showed me that even from the ashes of devastation, resilience could bloom. The past, although ever-present, no longer held me captive. I had finally started to truly rebuild, to truly live again.

Confronting Frank

The gravel crunched under my boots as I approached the weathered farmhouse, its paint peeling like sunburnt skin. It hadn't changed much since we'd lived here, a stark contrast to the upheaval in my own life. Frank's pickup truck sat in the yard, a rusting monument to our shared past. Taking a deep breath, I straightened my shoulders, the familiar weight of my concealed firearm a small comfort in the rising tide of apprehension. This wasn't about the law; this was personal.

He was waiting for me on the porch, a worn rocking chair creaking in rhythm with his nervous energy. He hadn't aged well. The sharp lines of his face were etched deeper, the vibrant blue eyes now shadowed with a weariness that mirrored my own. He looked up as I approached, his gaze lingering on my face, searching for something I wasn't sure I could provide.

"Laila," he said, his voice rough, almost a whisper. The name, once a caress, now felt like a brand.

"Frank," I replied, my tone flat, devoid of emotion. I kept my distance, maintaining a tactical awareness that years of training ingrained in me.

He didn't offer a chair. We stood facing each other, the silence thick with unspoken words, unresolved conflicts, the ghost of a love that had burned bright and then imploded.
The air hung heavy with the scent of pine and something else – regret, maybe. Or perhaps the smell of his pipe tobacco, a scent that once held a nostalgic comfort but now only reminded me of the suffocating claustrophobia of our marriage.
"I… I wanted to apologize," he finally said, his gaze falling to his hands. He picked at a loose thread on his worn denim shirt, a nervous tic I remembered well.

The apology hung in the air, incomplete, insufficient. Years of resentment, of betrayal, of the slow, agonizing unraveling of our relationship, couldn't be condensed into a single, mumbled sentence. "For what, Frank?" I asked, my voice even, controlled.

He looked up, his eyes meeting mine. "For everything. For hurting you. For being… selfish." His voice cracked, the admission a painful tremor in the still air.

"Selfish is an understatement," I said, my voice low but firm. The years of training kept my body rigid and calm. "You were reckless, Frank. You put us both in danger." The memory of the night the cartel attacked our safe house in Norway, the night our lives splintered into a thousand pieces, flashed through my mind. The image of his blood still sent a jolt through me.

He flinched. "I know. I made mistakes. Terrible mistakes. I was young, stupid. I thought…" He trailed off, unable to finish the thought.

"Thought what?" I pressed, wanting to force him to articulate the justifications, the rationalizations, that had driven his choices. The unspoken words had festered for too long.

"I thought I could handle it," he said, his voice barely above a whisper. "I thought I could protect you." He looked up, his eyes pleading. "I never wanted to hurt you, Laila. Never."

I didn't believe him, not fully. His "protection" had led to chaos, to betrayal. His actions had far exceeded their intentions. The consequences of his recklessness were etched onto my soul, a permanent scar.

"You wanted the excitement, Frank," I said,

my voice hard. “The thrill of the chase. You were chasing a ghost, a phantom ideal of your own creation. And in the process, you lost yourself, and you lost me.”

He nodded slowly, his gaze fixed on the worn wooden floorboards. The silence stretched, heavy and suffocating. He seemed to be wrestling with something inside, a battle between remorse and self-justification. I waited, my patience thin, but my resolve unwavering. I wouldn't leave until I had faced him, until I had confronted the man he was, the man he had become, and the devastation he had wrought.

Finally, he looked up, his eyes filled with a raw, unfiltered pain. “I know I can’t undo what I’ve done,” he said, his voice choked with emotion. “But I wanted you to know… I’m sorry.” His apology was different this time – sincere, lacking the pretense of the previous attempt. It was raw, and it was painful.

“Sorry doesn’t fix it, Frank,” I said, my voice still cold, yet my tone softening slightly. “It never will.” But I knew, deep down, that his apology, as inadequate as it was, was a step toward healing, not just for him, but for me. The weight of his confession had a strange, almost cathartic effect.

We talked for hours, the sun descending, casting long shadows across the yard. He spoke of his regrets, his mistakes, the burden he'd carried since the night everything fell apart. He spoke of the guilt, the self-loathing, the fear that he'd never be able to atone for what he'd done. He

spoke of the pain, the loneliness. The man he had become was a shadow of the man I had loved.

I listened, not with sympathy, not entirely, but with a detached curiosity, a professional assessment of the man before me. I saw the vulnerability beneath the bravado, the desperation behind his remorse. I recognized the familiar symptoms of post-traumatic stress disorder, the same silent battle I had been fighting. My own struggles provided a prism through which I could view his, a shared understanding, a mutual recognition of the pain that permeated our lives.

As darkness descended, a profound sadness settled between us. It was not the sadness of anger or resentment, but a deeper sorrow, a mutual understanding of the irrevocable choices we had made. It was the shared sorrow of a failed relationship, a shattered dream.

When I finally left, the air felt lighter, the weight of the unresolved past somehow lessened. It wasn't closure in the sense of a perfect resolution, a fairytale ending. There was no magical reconciliation, no sudden resurgence of love. But there was acceptance, an acknowledgment of the past, a recognition of the pain, a mutual understanding of the devastating consequences of their actions. The scars would remain, but the wound had finally begun to heal. The road to healing was still long, but I had taken a significant step, confronting not just my ex-husband, but the ghosts of our past. The silence of the drive back to the farm was not empty but filled with a sense of strange, unexpected peace. It was a beginning.

Dealing with Grief

The flickering candlelight cast long shadows across the worn wooden table in the small, sparsely furnished room I'd commandeered at the local motel. The air hung heavy with the scent of stale coffee and something else – the metallic tang of blood, a phantom smell clinging to my clothes, my skin, my very soul. The operation was over. The terrorists were apprehended, the potential massacre averted. But the victory felt hollow, the taste of success ashen in my mouth.
The faces of the fallen officers – their broken bodies, the silent screams frozen on their faces – haunted my every waking moment.

I stared at the single photograph resting on the table, a worn picture of Officer Miller, his kind eyes twinkling, his arm slung around his young daughter. He was barely older than I was. He had a future. Now there was only a photograph, a painful reminder of what was lost. The weight of his death, the weight of all the deaths, settled heavily upon me. I had trained for this, prepared for the brutality of violence, but the raw, unfiltered grief hit harder than any bullet ever had.

The rhythmic ticking of the cheap motel clock mocked my stillness, each tick a sharp, painful reminder of the relentless march of time. Time moved on, oblivious to the shattered lives left in its wake. Time moved on, even though a piece of me was forever frozen in the moment of carnage. The chilling echoes of gunshots still reverberated in my ears; the guttural screams of terror still clawed at my throat. My body was physically exhausted, but my mind was a battlefield, a chaotic landscape of trauma and sorrow.

My hands trembled as I reached for the worn, leather-bound journal I kept, its pages filled with tactical notes, observations, and the occasional, fleeting glimpse into the turbulent landscape of my inner world. I flipped through the pages, pausing at a particular entry from my time in Norway, a poignant entry detailing the loss of a comrade during a particularly brutal mission. The entry spoke of the searing pain, the numbness, the haunting silence that followed the deafening chaos. It was a mirror to my current state, a chilling reflection of my own grief.

The words I wrote then echoed now, resonating with a painful familiarity.

The silence after the storm is the worst. It's the silence of absence, the silence of what will never be again. The silence that screams louder than any explosion.

Sleep offered no respite. Nightmares clawed at the edges of my consciousness, relentless replays of the operation, the horrific details heightened, twisted, amplified. I would jolt awake, gasping for air, my heart hammering against my ribs, drenched in a cold sweat, the phantom sensations of the violence etched into my body. The smells and sounds were visceral, inescapable. I often ended up pacing the room until dawn, fueled by strong coffee and the haunting memories.
Every sound, every shadow, evoked fresh waves of terror and grief.

During the day, I tried to maintain a semblance of normalcy, a facade of strength and competence. I spoke with the families of the fallen officers, offering condolences, sharing stories of their bravery, of their unwavering dedication to duty. But behind the official facade, the weight of my own grief crushed me.

The polite smiles and carefully chosen words felt like a thin veil, a flimsy shield protecting the deep chasm of sorrow within. I found myself seeking solitude,
retreating into the shadows, allowing the grief to consume me.

The investigation continued. We pieced together the terrorist group's plans, their motives, their connections. We gathered evidence, interviewed witnesses, pieced together a timeline of their wicked scheme. But the task felt strangely detached from the raw reality of the loss. It felt like a mechanical process, a detached exercise in duty, devoid of the emotional depth of the reality.

The only solace I found was in the mundane tasks of daily life. The act of preparing simple meals, the repetitive actions of cleaning my apartment, and the calming rhythm of tending to my small herb garden became anchors in the swirling vortex of grief. These simple acts, devoid of the complexity of the events, provided an unexpected calm.
They were acts of normalcy within the extraordinary weight of the experience.

One evening, I found myself at the local cemetery, kneeling before Officer Miller's freshly turned grave. The crisp autumn air filled my lungs, a bittersweet reminder of the changing seasons. The gentle wind rustled the leaves, whispering secrets only the dead could understand. I placed a single white rose on the grave, a small gesture of respect, of mourning. I didn't speak, I didn't cry. The tears had long since dried up. But a profound sense of empathy resonated in the silence, a shared understanding of loss and sacrifice.

As I stood there, gazing across the rows of headstones, a strange sense of peace began to settle over me. It wasn't a happy peace, not a triumphant peace. It was a mournful peace, an acceptance of the irrevocable loss. It was the beginning of healing, a journey towards finding a way to carry the burden of grief without allowing it to crush me.

The grief wouldn't disappear. It would always be a part of me, a constant companion. But I would learn to live with it, to carry it with the strength and resilience forged in the fires of my past experiences. I would find my way through this darkness, not alone, but surrounded by the memories of those I had lost, and strengthened by the memories of those I had saved. The fight was far from over, but I had found the resolve, the inner strength, to keep going. I would honor their memories by continuing to fight, to protect the innocent, to uphold the law, even amidst the pain, even amidst the grief.

The road to healing would be long and arduous. The scars would remain, visible reminders of the horrors witnessed. But I would walk that road with purpose, with determination, with an unwavering commitment to making sure their sacrifices did not go in vain. The fallen officers would become my silent companions, their memory fueling my resolve. Their sacrifices would inspire me, bolster me, and provide the strength to confront the darkness that lurked in the shadows. The weight of grief would remain, but it would not define me. I would define my grief. I would forge my path forward, one step at a time, until I found a new measure of peace within the ongoing struggle. The sun set on another day, casting a long, final shadow over the cemetery, and I knew this was not the end, but a new beginning.

Rebuilding Relationships

The drive back to my family's farm felt longer than it should have. The familiar Pennsylvania landscape, usually a source of comfort, blurred into an indistinct green and brown tapestry. My mind, still reeling from the events of the past few days, replayed the faces of the fallen officers, their families' grief echoing in my ears. The victory felt hollow, a bitter pill swallowed in the face of such profound loss. I needed to ground myself, to reconnect with something real, something… stable. And that something was home.

My family had always been my anchor, my unwavering support system. But years of dedicated service, followed by a messy divorce, had created a chasm between us. Frank, my ex-husband, had been a soldier too, part of the elite Forsvarets Special Kommando in Norway. We'd met during a joint operation years ago; our shared experiences forging a bond that was both intense and ultimately fragile. The divorce had been brutal, a battlefield fought not with weapons, but with accusations and silent resentments. The distance between us had become an insurmountable wall, built brick by painful brick of unspoken words and unhealed wounds.

My parents greeted me with a mixture of relief and apprehension. The news of the terrorist attack had shaken them to their core; they had watched me on the news, their faces etched with worry. My mother, ever practical, had already prepared a pot of her famous chicken soup, a familiar comfort food that always seemed to soothe my soul, even in the face of the most turbulent storms.

The quiet supper was filled with unspoken anxieties. My father, a man of few words, kept casting concerned glances my way. My mother, ever watchful, subtly altered the conversation, steering it away from the traumatic events I had witnessed. The unspoken understanding hung heavy in the air, a silent acknowledgment of the grief we all shared. The usual banter was absent, replaced by a fragile, tentative peace. The silence, however, wasn't uncomfortable. It was a quiet space that allowed the unspoken emotions to breathe.

Later that evening, I sought out my younger sister, Sarah. Sarah, ten years my junior, had always looked up to me, idolizing my military career. But the distance created by my life in the service and my subsequent divorce had strained our relationship. She'd always been a free spirit, an artist; my rigid discipline and structured existence felt worlds away from her whimsical nature. We were kindred spirits bound by blood but estranged by life's paths.

Finding her in her studio, surrounded by canvases and paintbrushes, I sat beside her, watching her work. The colors on the palette seemed to mirror the chaotic landscape of my own emotions. Her artistic expression, once a source of frustration to me, now seemed like a poignant reflection of her resilience, her ability to transform chaos into beauty.

"How are you doing, sis?" she asked, her voice soft, her eyes filled with a concern that transcended our past disagreements.

The question, simple as it was, brought a fresh wave of emotion to the surface. The carefully constructed walls I'd erected to protect myself began to crumble. The tears that had been dammed up for days finally broke through, leaving me sobbing uncontrollably. Sarah didn't speak. She simply wrapped her arms around me, holding me close, providing a comfort that went beyond words.

It wasn't a magical healing, no sudden resolution of our differences. But it was a beginning. A starting point in a journey towards rebuilding the broken bridges. Over the next few days, I found myself confiding in Sarah, sharing details of the operation that I had kept locked inside. Her gentle presence, her empathy, allowed me to process my trauma in a way that I hadn't been able to do on my own.

Rebuilding the relationship with my parents proved more challenging. My father, a stoic figure who rarely expressed his emotions, found it difficult to articulate his feelings. His displays of affection were subtle, his actions spoke louder than words. He helped me with tasks around the farm, his quiet presence a constant reassurance. My mother, on the other hand, was more overtly affectionate. She tended to my wounds, both physical and emotional, with the unwavering love and care only a mother could provide. The unconditional support of my family, even with their own limitations in expression, became my lifeline.

The healing process was not linear; there were setbacks, moments of intense grief that threatened to engulf me. But the presence of my family, their unwavering love and support, provided the emotional anchor I desperately needed. The farm became a sanctuary, a place where I could heal, regroup and reconnect with a life that existed before the chaos of the operation.

Slowly, painstakingly, I began to mend the fractured pieces of my relationships. Regular calls with my closest friends, officers from my past service, became my lifeline to the outside world. They understood the toll that my line of work took; they understood the weight of the trauma that I carried.

They offered their support, their friendships providing a sense of camaraderie and belonging that helped me to feel less isolated. They were a crucial part of my support system.

One evening, while tending to my small herb garden, a familiar figure emerged from the shadows of the barn. Frank. The sight of him sent a wave of conflicting emotions through me. Anger, resentment, and a flicker of something else— longing?—warred within me. We stood in silence for a long moment, the air thick with unspoken words and unresolved issues.

The conversation wasn't easy. It was a painful excavation of old wounds, a confrontation with the ghosts of our past. But there was also a newfound honesty, a willingness to confront the pain and acknowledge our shared history. The years of silence, the unspoken resentments, began to melt away. We talked about our time in Norway, the shared experiences that had forged our bond. We revisited the memories, the good and the bad, acknowledging the roles both of us played in the failure of our relationship.

The conversation didn't magically erase the pain or mend our broken marriage. But it marked a turning point, a step towards understanding and reconciliation. It was a painful step, one fraught with emotional pitfalls and old wounds. But it was a step nonetheless, a testament to the resilience of the human spirit and the healing power of honest communication. It was a beginning, a tentative bridging of the chasm that had separated us. The road to healing is long, but it's a road I would begin to walk, not alone, but surrounded by the love and support of those closest to me. The future remained uncertain, but for the first time in a long time, I felt a glimmer of hope, a faint light piercing the darkness. The path to healing was long and winding, but with my family and my friends by my side, I was ready to

face it head-on. The journey to rebuild the fragments of my life had started, and I had faith that I would find my way through the turmoil and the chaos to the light at the other end.

Finding Peace

The days that followed were a blur of quiet moments and unexpected breakthroughs. The farm, once a symbol of a life I'd left behind, became my refuge, a place where the echoes of gunfire and the screams of the dying were slowly muted by the chirping of crickets and the rustling of leaves. Sleep remained elusive, haunted by fragmented images of the attack – the flashing lights, the twisted metal, the sheer terror in the eyes of the fallen officers. But within the comforting embrace of my family's home, I began to find a rhythm, a semblance of normalcy in the midst of the chaos.

My mother's chicken soup, a familiar comfort, became a ritual, a small act of self-care amidst the overwhelming emotional toll. The scent of simmering broth, the warmth of the steaming bowl, it grounded me, pulling me back from the precipice of despair. My father, ever stoic, found ways to show his love, his quiet presence a constant reassurance.

He'd fix a broken fence post, mend a leaky roof, his hands working diligently, his actions speaking louder than words. He understood the language of silence, the shared grief that didn't require articulation.

Sarah, my vibrant, artistic sister, became an unlikely confidante. Her art, once a source of mild contention between us, became a mirror reflecting the turbulence within me. She didn't offer platitudes or solutions; she simply listened, her presence offering an unwavering support that allowed me to unpack the trauma at my own pace. We spent hours in her studio, surrounded by canvases splashed with vibrant colors and hues that mirrored the complexities of my emotional landscape. Sometimes we'd talk, other times we'd sit in comfortable silence, each of us lost in our own world yet somehow connected through the shared bond of sisterhood. The chasm between us, once seemingly insurmountable, slowly began to shrink, replaced by a newfound understanding and empathy.

The healing process, however, wasn't linear. There were days when the grief threatened to overwhelm me, days when the memories of the attack came crashing back, vivid and agonizing. I'd find myself staring blankly into space, the sounds of the world fading into a muted hum as my mind replayed the horror. On those days, the familiar comfort of the farm became a shield, a sanctuary where I could retreat and process the pain without the judgment of the outside world. I'd spend hours tending to my herb garden, the repetitive act of weeding and watering a calming rhythm in the storm. The earthy scent of the soil, the feel of the cool damp soil between my fingers – it was a grounding force, anchoring me to the present moment, pulling me back from the abyss.

My friends, my fellow officers, became a lifeline, a crucial part of my support system. Regular phone calls, filled with shared laughter and understanding, helped to bridge the distance between my rural haven and the world I had left behind. They were the ones who truly understood the weight of my experiences, the invisible wounds that only those who have served could comprehend. They didn't preach platitudes or offer easy solutions; they simply listened, offering their support without judgment. They understood the long road ahead, the ongoing battle with PTSD and the lingering trauma. Their unwavering solidarity was a powerful antidote to the isolation that threatened to engulf me. Their stories, their shared experiences, their unwavering belief in my strength – it all became a source of both strength and comfort.

One evening, while stargazing in the vast expanse of the Pennsylvania night sky, a wave of unexpected calm washed over me. The countless stars, twinkling like distant embers, seemed to mirror the myriad memories that swirled within me. It wasn't a sudden resolution, not a magical healing, but a shift in perspective. The terror of the attack hadn't vanished, but its power over me had lessened. The memories remained, but they no longer held me captive. They were now part of my story, not my defining feature. I had survived. I had fought. I had won. And now, I was beginning to live again.

The wounds were deep, the scars would remain, but the sharp edges were beginning to soften. I learned to navigate the triggers, the sudden bursts of anxiety, the sleepless nights, the flashbacks. I learned to lean on my support system, to allow myself to be vulnerable, to accept the help that was offered. The path to healing was long and arduous, but it was a path I was walking, not alone, but surrounded by the love and support of my family and friends.

The process wasn't always easy. There were moments of doubt, of intense self-questioning, days when the darkness threatened to overwhelm the light. But I learned to embrace the discomfort, to recognize the setbacks as part of the journey, not as failures. I found strength in the small victories, in the quiet moments of peace, in the gentle smiles of my family, in the comforting words of my friends. It was a slow, painstaking process, a gradual unwinding of the trauma. But each day brought me closer to a sense of wholeness, a sense of acceptance.

The farm, once a reminder of the life I had left behind, became a symbol of my resilience, my strength, my ability to find peace amidst the chaos. It was here, surrounded by the familiar sights and sounds of nature, that I began to rebuild

my life, piece by piece, brick by painful brick. The journey was far from over, the scars remained, but the light at the end of the tunnel, once a distant glimmer, now shone brighter, promising a future where peace and acceptance wouldn't be a distant dream, but a tangible reality. The healing wasn't complete; it was an ongoing process, a testament to the human spirit's remarkable ability to endure, adapt and find a way to flourish even after facing the deepest darkness. The farm, my family, my friends – they were the beacons that guided me through the storm, the anchors that held me steadfast even when the winds of adversity threatened to tear me asunder. And in the quiet moments, amidst the gentle rustling of leaves, I found a sense of peace I hadn't known existed before. The battle was over; the war within was still being fought, but I was winning.

Acceptance and Moving Forward

The crisp autumn air carried the scent of woodsmoke and decaying leaves, a fragrance that once evoked a sense of melancholic longing now held a comforting familiarity. The farm, once a symbol of a life I'd left behind, had become my sanctuary, a place where the ghosts of my past were slowly losing their power. The relentless pursuit of justice, the adrenaline-fueled chases, the brutal hand-to-hand combat – all seemed distant echoes now, replaced by the gentle rhythm of rural life. I still carried the scars, both visible and invisible, but they no longer defined me. They were a testament to my resilience, a reminder of my strength.

My days unfolded in a predictable, soothing rhythm. Mornings began with the crowing of roosters and the gentle mooing of cows, a far cry from the jarring sounds of sirens and gunfire that once dominated my reality. I found solace in tending to my father's garden, the repetitive act of weeding and planting a meditative practice that helped calm the turmoil within. The soil, rich and dark, offered a grounding presence, connecting me to the earth and to something larger than my personal struggles. The vibrant colors of the blooming sunflowers, a stark contrast to the muted grays and blacks of my memories, offered a subtle but potent reminder of life's enduring beauty.

Evenings were spent with my family, sharing meals, recounting stories, and simply enjoying each other's company. My relationship with my brother, Daniel, had blossomed into something unexpected – a genuine camaraderie born from shared experiences and unspoken understanding. We'd spend hours in his studio, surrounded by her vibrant canvases, a silent conversation unfolding

between us, the paint strokes mirroring the complexities of our emotions. He still found my military past unsettling at times, a stark contrast to his peaceful artistic world he found, but there was a newfound appreciation, a respect for the strength I'd found within myself. Our bond, strengthened by our shared grief and subsequent healing, was something I never expected, a treasure I fiercely protected.

My mother's chicken soup, once a simple comfort food, became a symbol of my journey towards healing. Each spoonful was a small act of self-care, a reminder that even in the midst of adversity, there was still space for simple joys and comforting routines. My deceased father, ever stoic, would have offered his quiet support, his unspoken love still a constant presence in my life. Their silent understanding was a comfort, a testament to the enduring power of family.

The memories of the attack, once overwhelmingly vivid, now faded into the background, although they remained a part of who I was. The faces of the fallen officers, their haunted eyes reflecting their fear, still lingered in my thoughts, but they no longer held the power to paralyze me. The grief was a constant companion, an undercurrent in the gentle flow of my daily life. But it had lost its sharp edge, becoming a dull ache that I could manage, accept, even live with. I learned to embrace the memories, not as a burden, but as a part of my story, a reminder of my resilience, of my ability to overcome great challenges.

My friends from the force, my brothers and sisters in arms, remained a vital part of my support system. Regular phone calls, shared laughter, and quiet moments of understanding kept the bond strong across the miles that separated us. They understood the invisible wounds, the lingering trauma, the constant battle against PTSD that often threatened to overwhelm me. Their stories, their unwavering support, their faith in my ability to heal, were invaluable gifts, keeping me grounded and reminding me that I was not alone. They understood the process, the setbacks, the moments of darkness and self-doubt that were part and parcel of healing. They were a lifeline, a constant source of strength.

I found solace in unexpected places – in the rhythmic chirping of crickets, in the gentle rustle of leaves, in the vast expanse of the night sky speckled with countless stars.
Nature, once a distant background, had become my teacher, a silent witness to my healing journey. I learned to listen to its whispers, to find a sense of peace in its unchanging rhythms. The gentle swaying of the tall grass in the wind, the comforting warmth of the sun on my skin – they became anchors that rooted me in the present moment.

The process of healing wasn't linear; it was a labyrinthine journey with unexpected twists and turns. There were days when the darkness threatened to consume me, days when the memories of the attack came crashing back with full force, making it impossible to breathe. But I persevered. I learned to identify my triggers, to manage my reactions, to embrace the discomfort. I leaned on my support system, allowing myself to be vulnerable, to accept help when it was offered. I acknowledged the setbacks as part of the journey, not as failures. The small victories – a peaceful night's sleep, a productive day in the garden, a heartfelt laugh with my sister – were celebrated as triumphs.

Acceptance, I realized, wasn't about forgetting or erasing the past. It was about acknowledging the pain, the trauma, the losses, and integrating them into the fabric of my life without letting them define me. It was about finding a way to live alongside the memories, to honor the fallen, and to carry
their sacrifice with me as a source of strength and inspiration.

As the seasons changed, so did I. The sharp edges of my grief began to soften, replaced by a quiet sense of acceptance. The farm, once a place of bittersweet memories, now held a sense of peace and belonging. It was a testament to my resilience, a symbol of my journey towards healing.
The scars remained, visible reminders of the battles fought and won, but they were also badges of honor, proof of my strength. The path to healing, I knew, was an ongoing journey, not a destination. But I was walking

it, step by steady step, towards a brighter future. The war within might not be entirely over, but I had gained a decisive advantage, and the end was in sight. The future held uncertainty, yes, but there was also a palpable sense of hope, a quiet confidence that I would navigate whatever challenges lay ahead. The possibilities were endless, and for the first time since the attack, I was excited to see what life held next.

A New Assignment

The phone call came on a Tuesday, the kind of unremarkable day that blurred into the others, punctuated only by the rhythmic chirping of crickets and the distant lowing of cows. It was Agent Miller, his voice a familiar rumble across the miles, a voice that carried the weight of shared experiences and unspoken understanding. He didn't beat around the bush, not Miller. Straight to the point, always.

"Laila," he said, his voice a low baritone, "We have a new assignment for you. Something… delicate."

Delicate. The word hung in the air, heavy with unspoken implications. Delicate meant dangerous. Delicate meant high stakes. Delicate meant my skills, my experience, the very essence of my being would be tested yet again. A familiar thrill, a cocktail of adrenaline and apprehension, coursed through my veins. The quiet peace of the Pennsylvania countryside seemed to fade, replaced by the phantom echo of sirens and the metallic tang of blood.

I took a deep breath, trying to anchor myself in

the present. The scent of woodsmoke and decaying leaves still hung in the air, a gentle counterpoint to the rising storm within. “Tell me,” I said, my voice calm, controlled, despite the turmoil raging inside.

Miller paused, a brief silence stretching between us, thick with anticipation. “It’s in the Pacific Northwest,” he began, “A series of seemingly unrelated incidents, but we believe they’re connected. Smuggling, you see, but not the kind you’d expect. Something far more… sophisticated.”

“Sophisticated how?” I pressed, the hunter’s instinct taking over, my mind already dissecting the fragments of information, building a picture from the shadows. My life, for better or worse, had become an intricate dance of anticipation and reaction. A life spent chasing shadows and dealing with danger.

“High-tech weaponry. Advanced surveillance. We suspect a connection to a group we’ve been tracking for some time. A shadowy organization operating on a global scale. Their reach stretches far beyond the initial smuggling, Laila. This is about much more than just weapons and profit. This… this could unravel the fabric of society. And we need you.”

My past resurfaced, not in waves of trauma, but in a surge of controlled excitement, a familiar fire reignited in my soul.
The years spent in the Army Rangers, the precision of my movements, the honed instincts, the lethal efficiency of my training, all surged to the forefront of my consciousness. The memories of Norway, of my time with the Forsvarets Special Kommando, the bond forged in blood and shared sacrifice, the love I'd felt for Frank during those dangerous times. The weight of my past experiences, good and bad, fuelled me.
This was where I belonged. This was what I was made for.

"What kind of weaponry?" I asked, my voice neutral, betraying none of the exhilaration coursing through me. The thrill of the hunt, the intellectual challenge, the sheer adrenaline – all of it was intoxicating. This wasn't just a job; it was a calling. This was a chance to use the skills that were a part of my very being.

"We're still piecing it together," Miller admitted. "But initial reports suggest something… unconventional. Something that could be extremely disruptive, with potentially catastrophic consequences."

“And what about my civilian life? The farm? My family?” I asked, the question a necessary ritual, a formality to acknowledge the life I was leaving behind, even if only temporarily. The life I had fought so hard to rebuild. The peace I had craved, the tranquility I had found.

“We’ll take care of things here,” he assured me. “Your family’s safety is paramount. This won’t be a long-term deployment, Laila. We’re just…” he paused, searching for the right words, “We’re just trying to neutralize the threat as quickly as possible.”

“And what’s the timeline?”

“As soon as possible. We’ve already arranged a flight for tomorrow morning.”

Tomorrow morning. The suddenness of it sent a jolt of adrenaline through me. I was accustomed to living on the edge, but the transition from peaceful rural life to the chaos of a high-stakes investigation always created a disconcerting imbalance. The shift was jarring, a whiplash of emotions – a nostalgic tenderness for the simple joys of life, punctuated by the sharp excitement of impending danger. I felt the tug of two worlds, two opposing forces, pulling at me from opposite ends.

I spent the rest of the day preparing, a whirlwind of activity designed to create an illusion of control in the face of impending chaos. Packing my bag felt oddly symbolic, each item a reminder of my past life, my present situation, and my uncertain future. My trusty Glock 19, a familiar weight in my hand, reassuring, comforting. My specialized knives and tactical gear, neatly organized in my military backpack, each piece a testament to years of rigorous training. Spare magazines, tactical pens, emergency supplies, all carefully inventoried and checked. The ritual was familiar, almost comforting; a sense of order in the face of an impending storm.

There was a strange sense of finality as I packed the small box of photos from my time in Norway. Memories, smiles, adventures. A lifetime in a few snapshots. I closed the box gently, placing it carefully inside my bag. It was a reminder of my past, of who I was, and of what I was capable of. My past experiences would serve as my guide, my support system, the fuel for the challenges that lay ahead.

I made a point of saying goodbye to my family, each hug a silent promise of my return. My mother's embrace held a quiet strength, a confidence that belied her worry. My father's

stoic silence spoke volumes, his unspoken love a constant source of strength. Sarah's artistic nature displayed itself in the vibrant flower painting she placed in my bag, a burst of color against the harsh reality of the coming days. They understood, in their own way, the nature of my work, the need to chase shadows, to bring the darkness to light.
They understood that this was a part of me, an integral part of who I was.

The next morning, I found myself standing at the edge of a new beginning, a new chapter in my life. The crisp morning air held a promise of adventure, tinged with the ever-present knowledge of danger. I was on my way, not just to a new assignment, but to a journey into the unknown, a leap of faith, a commitment to face my destiny, whatever it might bring. The sun rose, casting long shadows across the landscape, mirroring the uncertainty of the path ahead. But this time, unlike the funeral I attended so long ago, I was not in mourning. I felt a growing sense of anticipation, a sense that the journey would lead me to new truths, to greater
understanding, to new challenges that would test my limits, my skills, and my endurance.

The plane ride was long, but the anticipation kept me awake. I spent most of the time reviewing the intel, the scant information Miller had provided, piecing together the fragments like a puzzle. Each piece of information fit into the larger picture, creating a sharper, clearer image of the danger ahead. This was not a routine smuggling operation; the stakes were much higher, the implications far more profound than initially suggested. This was a battle for the very fabric of society. I could feel the weight of the world resting on my shoulders, but instead of fear, I felt a growing sense of determination. I was ready. I was prepared. I was Laila Aurora Wright, former Army Ranger, now U.S. Marshal, and I was going to stop them.

Returning to Duty

The Seattle airport was a whirlwind of activity, a stark contrast to the quiet solitude of the Pennsylvania farm. The air hung thick with the scent of coffee and jet fuel, a pungent aroma that always seemed to accompany the beginning of a new mission. Agent Miller met me at baggage claim, his presence as familiar and comforting as a well-worn boot. He was a man of few words, but his eyes, sharp and perceptive, spoke volumes. They held the quiet understanding of a shared past, a brotherhood forged in the crucible of danger.

"The safe house is secure," he said, his voice low, barely audible above the airport's noise. "Everything is ready."

The car ride was a blur of city lights and late-night traffic. Seattle at night held a different kind of beauty, a raw, untamed energy that mirrored the urgency of the mission. The safe house was a nondescript apartment in a quiet residential neighborhood, nothing flashy, nothing that would attract unwanted attention. It was functional, efficient, a place designed for work, not comfort. The essentials were there – a computer with secure access, a satellite phone, a small arsenal of weapons discreetly tucked away. Everything I needed. Nothing I didn't.

The briefing was concise and to the point. Miller laid out the details of the operation, a meticulously assembled tapestry woven from fragments of intelligence. The group, known only as "The Architects," were masterminds of technological warfare, specializing in the development and distribution of advanced weaponry. Their operations were shrouded in secrecy, their reach extending across continents. Their motives were still unclear, but the consequences of their actions were devastatingly clear.

"We've traced their activities to a series of seemingly unrelated incidents," Miller explained, gesturing to a map spread out on the table. "Smuggling operations, cyberattacks, even targeted assassinations. But they're all connected. It's a coordinated effort, a carefully orchestrated campaign designed to destabilize key sectors of the global economy."

He pointed to a specific location on the map, a secluded warehouse district on the outskirts of Seattle. "This is their primary hub," he continued. "We believe they're planning something big, something that could have catastrophic consequences. We need to stop them before they can execute their plan."

The information Miller provided was like a puzzle, the pieces scattered and incomplete, but with the potential to reveal a terrifyingly clear picture when pieced together. My mind worked in overdrive, my years of training kicking in, transforming the raw data into actionable intelligence. I began to see the patterns, the connections, the insidious logic behind the Architects' actions. This was far more than simple smuggling; this was a full-scale assault on global security. My gut told me this was bigger than I had first imagined. This felt personal.

The next few days were a whirlwind of activity. I spent countless hours studying satellite imagery, analyzing intercepted communications pouring over the latest intelligence reports. I worked with a small team of analysts, each a specialist in their field – cyber security, logistics, intelligence gathering. We were a well-oiled machine, each piece essential to the smooth functioning of the whole. The team respected my skills, my experience, my ability to see the larger picture. They trusted my judgment. The respect was mutual. This wasn't just a job; it was a shared purpose, a unified commitment to stopping the Architects.

My training, honed over years of service in the Army Rangers and the U.S. Marshals Service, proved invaluable. I could analyze situations, identify vulnerabilities, predict enemy movements with an accuracy that bordered on precognition. I could read people, see their tells, discern their true intentions even behind carefully constructed facades.
My time with the Forsvarets Special Kommando in Norway, those years spent living and fighting alongside Frank, had been instrumental in shaping my abilities, making me the formidable operative I was today. Those were the best of my years, but the worst too. I carried those scars, but they fueled me, made me stronger, sharper, more decisive.

The plan was meticulous, a carefully crafted strategy designed to minimize risk and maximize effectiveness. We would infiltrate the warehouse undetected, neutralize the threat, and seize the evidence. The risks were high, but the potential rewards far outweighed the dangers. The Architects had to be stopped, and it was up to us to do it. This wasn't just a matter of justice. It was about preventing a global catastrophe.

The night of the raid arrived like a predator stalking its prey. The city was dark, silent, save for the distant hum of traffic. My team and I moved with the precision of a well-oiled machine, our movements fluid, silent, deadly. We approached the warehouse, our senses heightened, our instincts sharp. The air was thick with anticipation, the tension palpable. This was it. The culmination of weeks of meticulous planning, relentless investigation, and unwavering dedication.

The infiltration was flawless. We moved through the shadows like ghosts, our movements undetectable. The warehouse was a maze of corridors, storage rooms, and hidden passageways, but we navigated it with ease, our knowledge of the layout precise, our movements precise. We encountered resistance, of course, but we were prepared. The ensuing firefight was brief, brutal, and efficient. We neutralized the threat, securing the warehouse and apprehending the perpetrators without casualties on our side.

The evidence we discovered was overwhelming. The Architects possessed an arsenal of advanced weaponry, enough to cause unimaginable damage. Their plans were far-reaching, their ambition terrifying. But we had stopped them. We had prevented a catastrophe.

The aftermath was a blur of paperwork, debriefings, and media coverage. My role in the operation remained confidential, but the satisfaction was immense. We had done our job, and we had done it well.

The quiet satisfaction of a mission accomplished settled over me as I boarded my flight back to Pennsylvania. The familiar landscape of rolling hills and green fields was a welcome sight. This time, returning home felt different. The adrenaline rush had faded, replaced by a quiet contentment, the satisfaction of a job well done. As the plane touched down, I felt a sense of closure, a sense of fulfillment. The past was behind me, but the future stretched ahead, promising more challenges, more adventures, more opportunities to put my skills to the test. I was Laila Aurora Wright, former Army Ranger, former U.S. Marshal, and I was ready for whatever came next. My journey was far from over. This was just the beginning. The world needed guardians, and I intended to continue to be one.

Facing the Future

The Pennsylvania farmhouse, usually a sanctuary of quietude, felt strangely vibrant after the intensity of the Seattle operation. The scent of freshly baked bread, a stark contrast to the metallic tang of gunpowder still clinging to my memory, filled the air. My sister, Sarah, her face etched with worry lines that I'd noticed deepening over the past few months, rushed to greet me. "Laila! You're back! Mom's been frantic." Her hug was tight, a physical manifestation of the unspoken anxieties that had been simmering between us since my departure.

The reunion with my mother was tender, tinged with a relieved exhaustion that we both silently shared. The distance between us, created by my career, my divorce, and the inherent secrecy that shrouded my life, had begun to feel insurmountable at times. Yet, in that embrace, the years seemed to melt away, replaced by an unbreakable bond. We had always been close, a silent understanding that transcended words. Her love was a constant, a grounding force in a life often defined by chaos.

The following days were spent reconnecting with the rhythm of farm life. The familiar chores—feeding the animals, tending the garden, the quiet satisfaction of making something grow from the earth—were a balm to my soul.

The simplicity of it all was a welcome contrast to the complexities of my work. Yet, the peace was a fragile thing, easily disrupted by the persistent echoes of the past. The memories of Frank, of our life together in Norway, clung to me like shadows, refusing to be banished.

The divorce had been brutal, a bitter end to a fiery love. We had met during my time with the Forsvarets Special Kommando, our shared experiences forging an intense bond that burned brightly, but eventually consumed itself. His death—a casualty of a mission gone wrong— had left a deep scar, a wound that refused to heal. The pain, though dulled by time, still lingered, a phantom limb that occasionally throbbed with a sharp, insistent ache.

Yet, amid the quiet solitude of the farm, I found a different kind of strength emerging. It wasn't the adrenaline-fueled intensity of combat, but a deeper, more enduring resilience. I realized I was no longer defined by my past, by the trauma, by the losses. I was more than my past experiences; I was the sum of my choices, my actions, my resilience. The farm became more than a sanctuary; it was a place of healing, growth, and self-discovery. The earth, as always, offered solace, a silent witness to my inner turmoil.

My work, however, was far from over. The victory against the Architects had been significant, but it was just one battle in a larger war. The world was a dangerous place, filled with threats both seen and unseen. The intelligence community contacted me several times, offering opportunities, consultations, and additional assignments. The allure of the chase, the adrenaline-pumping thrill of the operation, was tempting, but I hesitated.

I needed time, not just to rest, but to reflect, to decide what kind of life I wanted, what kind of legacy I wanted to leave. The farm was more than just a place to escape; it was a springboard for a new chapter in my life. I had spent so much time being Laila Aurora Wright, the highly skilled soldier and marshal, always on the go, always reacting. Now I needed to define Laila Aurora Wright, the woman.

The quiet solitude provided a clarity I hadn't had before. I began to recognize the patterns, not just in the chaos of espionage, but in my own life. I realized how my relentless pursuit of justice had obscured other important aspects of myself. I had become so focused on fighting the external battles that I had neglected my inner peace.

One evening, as the sun dipped below the horizon, painting the sky in hues of orange and purple, I sat on the porch swing, the gentle breeze rustling the leaves of the ancient oak trees. My thoughts drifted to the future, the possibilities that lay ahead. I knew there would be more challenges, more risks, more dangers. But I also knew I was stronger now, more resilient, more capable than ever before.

The Architects' operation had been a wake-up call. It had shown me the immense power of collaboration, the importance of trust, and the strength that comes from working together toward a common goal. I realized that I didn't have to fight alone. I had a network of friends, colleagues, and family who believed in me, who supported me, and who were willing to stand by me. This realization was deeply profound.

My past experiences in the Forsvarets Special

Kommando, the rigorous training, the harrowing missions—all of it had shaped me, molded me into the woman I was today. But I wasn't defined by those experiences. I was defined by my ability to learn, to adapt, to overcome. I had faced incredible challenges, and not just in my professional life. My personal struggles had tested me in ways that no battlefield ever could. Yet, through it all, I had persevered and emerged stronger.

The next morning, I woke with a renewed sense of purpose. The quiet contentment of farm life had provided the

necessary introspection. I had come to terms with my past and was ready to embrace the future. I decided to take up a part-time position as a consultant for the FBI, offering my specialized skills in a limited capacity. It was a balance I could maintain, allowing me to fulfill my need for action while enjoying the tranquility of rural life.

The transition was smoother than anticipated. The familiarity of the intelligence world, the camaraderie of my colleagues, and the challenging nature of the work provided a sense of continuity. Yet, the difference was significant. I was no longer consumed by the relentless pursuit of justice; instead, I was strategically guiding the fight. I wasn't just reacting; I was proactive.

I spent my days tending to my farm, connecting with my family, and occasionally lending my expertise to the FBI. It was a life that blended the best of both worlds, the adrenaline-fueled intensity of the past and the quiet serenity of the present. I had found a balance, a sense of harmony that I had previously craved.

Life wasn't devoid of challenges. There were still threats to combat, conspiracies to unravel, and justice to pursue. But now, I faced them with a renewed sense of purpose, a profound understanding of my strengths and weaknesses, and an unwavering commitment to balance. I was not merely a warrior, but a woman capable of adapting, evolving, and finding peace amid the storm.

The scars remained, a testament to my past struggles, but they were now a reminder of my resilience, my capacity for growth. I had learned to accept the past, not as a defining element, but as a stepping stone to a brighter future. This was a new beginning, a testament to my strength, my growth, and my ability to face whatever came next. The future, once a source of anxiety, now held a thrill of potential, a quiet confidence that I could conquer any challenges that lay ahead. I was Laila Aurora Wright, and this was my story, still unfolding, still being written, one chapter at a time.

Reflection on Growth

The rhythmic creak of the porch swing became a soundtrack to my introspection. The Pennsylvania evenings, once a backdrop to quiet contemplation, now served as a canvas for painting a new future. The scent of woodsmoke mingled with the sweet perfume of honeysuckle, a comforting aroma that grounded me in the present moment, a stark contrast to the harsh realities I had recently faced. The Seattle operation, while successful, had left its mark. It wasn't just the physical exhaustion, the adrenaline-induced tremors that lingered in my muscles; it was the emotional toll, the weight of responsibility, the constant awareness of the fragility of life.

I had faced death before, stared into the abyss of loss during my years with the Forsvarets Special Kommando. Frank's death, still a raw wound, had shaped me, forced me to confront my own mortality. But the Seattle incident was different. It wasn't the risk of my own demise that haunted me, it was the potential loss of innocent lives, the devastating consequences of failure. The thought of those innocents, caught in the crossfire of a terrorist plot, kept me awake at night. It was a burden I carried, a stark reminder of the human cost of conflict.

The quiet of the farm allowed me to process these emotions. It wasn't a retreat, but a strategic repositioning. I wasn't running away from my past; I was integrating it into my present, forging a future that honored my experiences without being defined by them. The farm, once a symbol of my past life with Frank, had transformed into a refuge, a sanctuary where I could reconnect with my roots, my family, and myself. The familiar rhythm of farm life – the gentle rise and fall of the sun, the changing seasons, the quiet predictability of nature – provided a counterpoint to the unpredictable world of espionage and law enforcement.

My work with the FBI had evolved too. My part-time consultancy allowed me to engage with the challenges I loved – the intellectual thrill of the chase, the satisfaction of using my skills to serve justice – without sacrificing the tranquility I had found on the farm. It was a carefully crafted balance, a delicate equilibrium that I guarded fiercely. The work itself had shifted from a frantic response to a more strategic approach. Instead of rushing headlong into danger, I was utilizing my experience to guide the FBI, shaping the direction of investigations, offering my expertise as a consultant, not as a soldier leading the charge. I could leverage my tactical knowledge, my experience in hostage negotiations and high-stakes operations, to help others navigate treacherous waters, but from a position of calculated strength.

There was a quiet satisfaction in this new role, a sense of fulfillment that went beyond the adrenaline rush of active duty. I was still making a difference, still using my skills to protect the innocent, but now I was also investing in myself, nurturing my well-being, and forging a more holistic sense of self. The clarity that had dawned in the peaceful solitude of the Pennsylvania countryside allowed me to approach my work with a renewed sense of focus and purpose. My priorities had shifted. The balance between my professional and personal life, once a distant dream, was now a tangible reality.

This newfound equilibrium didn't mean a life devoid of challenges. The threats were ever-present, the world remained a dangerous place, and the fight for justice never truly ceased. But my approach had changed. I was no longer solely reliant on brute force and raw adrenaline; I was adept at strategic thinking, leveraging my networks and resources to preempt threats, neutralize risks, and safeguard lives. I was learning to anticipate, to plan, and to build stronger, more resilient networks, both within the FBI and beyond.

The connections I had forged with colleagues, contacts, and even former adversaries, had become invaluable. The understanding of collaboration and the strength that came from trust was a cornerstone of my new approach. It was a powerful lesson learned in the crucible of Seattle, a realization that had transformed my perspective and empowered my strategies. I had learned the value of reaching out, of relying on the support and wisdom of others. The solitude of the farm had been crucial for introspection and healing, but the strength I now wielded wasn't born from isolation; it thrived on connection.

My past experiences, the rigorous training, the harrowing missions, the emotional scars – they were all part of my story, interwoven into the fabric of who I am. They had shaped me, honed my skills, forged my resilience. But they no longer defined me. I was more than the sum of my past experiences. I was a constantly evolving entity, shaped by my experiences but not constrained by them. I was learning to use my past as a springboard, not an anchor.

The scars remained, both physical and emotional, tangible reminders of the battles fought and won. They were not symbols of defeat, but badges of honor, proof of resilience, testament to my enduring strength. They were the etched lines on a map, charting the journey of a woman who had faced the darkest corners of the world and emerged into the light, transformed and empowered. The pain was still there, but it no longer controlled me. It had become a source of strength, a reminder of how far I had come, how much I had overcome.

The future was no longer an uncertain prospect; it was a tapestry of possibilities waiting to be woven. I was no longer simply reacting to the challenges that life threw my way; I was actively shaping my destiny. The quiet confidence that had bloomed in the solitude of the farmhouse had translated into a potent force, a driving energy that pushed me forward. I was Laila Aurora Wright, a woman who had learned to embrace both the quiet tranquility of rural life and the adrenaline-fueled intensity of the fight for justice, a woman who had found balance, harmony, and a profound sense of self. And this new beginning, this chapter in my life, was just the start. The story, far from over, was continuing, evolving, reaching towards a future that held both challenges and a quiet, deep satisfaction. The journey was far from over; in fact, it was only just beginning.

Epilogue: A New Threat

The rhythmic chirping of crickets replaced the porch swing's creak as autumn painted the Pennsylvania landscape in fiery hues. The quietude, once a balm to my soul, now felt pregnant with an unspoken tension. The Seattle case, the successful dismantling of the domestic terrorist cell, had felt like a definitive end, a closing of a chapter. But the silence held a disquieting undercurrent, a whisper of something unseen, something brewing just beneath the surface. It was a feeling I knew all too well, the prickling sensation of impending danger that ran colder than any autumn wind.

My FBI consultancy had become less about active engagements and more about strategic foresight. I found myself poring over intelligence reports, analyzing patterns, connecting seemingly disparate threads. The digital world had become my new battlefield, a virtual landscape where threats lurked behind encrypted messages and anonymous online forums. I was a silent guardian, a watchful sentinel, using my years of experience to identify and neutralize risks before they escalated into full-blown crises.

One late evening, while reviewing a series of seemingly innocuous online posts, a pattern emerged. It was subtle, almost imperceptible, a coded language only someone with my background could decipher. The posts, seemingly related to survivalist groups and prepping communities, contained hidden messages, coordinates, and veiled threats directed at specific targets – targets that included key figures in the law enforcement community.

The chilling realization hit me like a physical blow. This wasn't just some disgruntled fringe group venting online;

this was something far more organized, far more dangerous. These weren't isolated individuals; this was a network, a clandestine organization meticulously planning something far more sinister than the Seattle cell. Their reach was wider, their objectives more ambitious, and their methods more sophisticated. They weren't interested in symbolic acts of violence; they were planning a coordinated attack, a widespread assault targeting the very fabric of law enforcement.

My initial reaction was a surge of adrenaline, a familiar rush that pulled me back into the fight. But this time, the instinct to charge headlong into the fray was tempered by experience, by the lessons learned in Seattle, by the quiet wisdom gained from the tranquil solitude of the Pennsylvania farm. This time, I wouldn't rely solely on instinct and brute force. This required a different kind of strategy, a more nuanced approach.

I contacted Agent Miller, my primary contact at the FBI. He was skeptical at first, hesitant to take the online chatter seriously. He needed proof, concrete evidence to justify launching a full-scale investigation. But I had learned to trust my gut, to recognize the subtle signs of danger, the whispers before the storm. I presented him with my analysis, the decoded messages, the geographical coordinates, and the potential targets. He listened intently, his initial skepticism gradually replaced by a growing sense of unease.

The evidence was circumstantial, but it was enough to pique his interest. He agreed to a preliminary investigation, a discreet probe into the online activities and real-world connections of the individuals identified in my analysis. My role shifted from active participation to strategic guidance. I was the architect of the investigation, the unseen hand guiding the agents on the ground, providing insights and anticipating their moves.

The investigation stretched over weeks, a slow, methodical process of piecing together a puzzle of cryptic messages and fragmented clues. The online forums, once seemingly innocuous, now revealed a complex web of connections, a hidden network of individuals operating under a shared ideology. Their communication was sophisticated, using layers of encryption and employing techniques that made tracking them incredibly challenging.

As we delved deeper, the scale of the threat became horrifyingly clear. This wasn't just a group; it was a well- funded, well-organized network with access to weapons, training, and logistical support. Their objective was far-reaching, aimed at destabilizing the law enforcement infrastructure and sowing chaos across the nation. This wasn't merely a plot; it was a calculated campaign of terror.

The weight of responsibility pressed down on me, the familiar burden of knowing that countless lives were hanging in the balance. But unlike the Seattle operation, I didn't feel the pressure of being alone, of carrying the weight of the world on my shoulders. This time, I had a team, a network of skilled agents, dedicated professionals working alongside me, trusting my instincts and my expertise.

We worked tirelessly, building a case against this new threat. We infiltrated their online forums, gathered intelligence, and tracked their real-world movements. The evidence mounted, slowly but surely painting a picture of a coordinated attack targeting law enforcement agencies across the country. This was going to be a complex operation, requiring a multi-agency effort, a coordinated response involving local, state, and federal agencies.

The quiet solitude of the Pennsylvania farm, once a refuge, now served as a strategic command center. I used my knowledge of the terrain, my understanding of local dynamics, and my vast network of contacts to plan our counter-offensive. I coordinated with the FBI, sharing my intelligence and guiding the investigation, while simultaneously building a network of allies and contacts within local law enforcement communities.

The final confrontation wasn't a single, dramatic showdown. It was a series of carefully coordinated operations, swift and precise takedowns of key operatives, disruptions of communication networks, and the dismantling of their logistical infrastructure. It was a war fought not in the open battlefield, but in the shadows, a battle of wits and strategy, a game of cat and mouse across a vast digital and physical landscape.

The arrest of the key leaders marked the end of this phase, but the fight was far from over. The network was vast and its reach extended far beyond the individuals we had captured. There would be other cells, other operatives waiting in the wings. The threat had been neutralized, but it hadn't been eliminated. The seeds of discord had been sown, the undercurrents of discontent still simmered, waiting for the right moment to resurface.

As I watched the sun rise over the Pennsylvania fields, the same quiet peace returned, but it was different now. It wasn't the naive serenity of the past, but a calm born of experience, of understanding, of the quiet confidence that came from knowing that I had faced the darkness and emerged stronger, more resolute. The fight for justice was an unending war, a constant vigilance, a continuous battle against the forces of chaos and evil. It was a life I had chosen, a responsibility I embraced, not with blind courage, but with careful calculation and unwavering determination. This new beginning, this moment of peace, was not the end of the story, but a brief respite before the next chapter, the next threat, the next battle began. The game, it seemed, was far from over. The whispers were already starting again, faintly at first, but growing louder, hinting at new enemies, new challenges, and the persistent fight for a future where justice prevailed, even in the face of overwhelming odds. The quiet of the farm was a prelude, not an end. The fight, for me, was just beginning again.

Acknowledgments

First and foremost, I extend my deepest gratitude to my family and friends, whose unwavering support and patience made this book possible. Their understanding of the long hours and intense focus required for writing a project like this was invaluable.

I also want to thank my beta readers, "my amazing beta reader team", for their thorough reviews and constructive criticisms. Their insights were incredibly helpful in refining the plot, characters, and overall narrative.

Finally, a special thank you to the members of the Law enforcement community for their service and for inspiring many of the details in this novel.

Glossary

This glossary provides definitions for specialized terms used throughout the novel, primarily related to military tactics, law enforcement procedures, and the specific terminology of domestic terrorism.

Forsvarets Spesial kommando (FSK): The Norwegian military's special forces unit.

SWAT: Special Weapons and Tactics team.

EOD: Explosive Ordnance Disposal.

SIGINT: Signals Intelligence.

HUMINT: Human Intelligence.

OPSEC: Operations Security.

COMSEC: Communications Security.

Disclaimer

While this novel is a work of fiction, certain aspects of the narrative were informed by real-world events and research.

The novel's plot and characters are primarily fictional creations, and any resemblance to real persons, living or dead, is purely coincidental.

About the Author

A native of New York City growing up in Boston, E.S. Bennett has always had a passion for storytelling and has been refining his craft for 40 years. Most of his writing has been influenced by strong women in his life. He looks at them as major influences.

This is their First novel. They currently reside in North Carolina.

www.ingramcontent.com/pod-product-compliance
Lightning Source LLC
Chambersburg PA
CBHW070639310726
48982CB00001B/335
* 9 7 9 8 2 1 8 9 9 7 3 3 5 *